"Oh, my God," she whispered and pushed him away. **"What are you doing?"** she said, her hand hovering near her mouth, her eyes wild and accusing.

"If you don't know, apparently I wasn't doing it right."

"Don't get cute! You know what I'm talking about!" She ran her hands through her shoulder-length hair and paced around the room. She stopped and glared at him. "I don't know what possessed you to kiss me, but you'd better make sure it doesn't happen again!"

"I'm attracted to you and, based on that kiss, I'd say the feelings are mutual. So I did what I've longed to do for years. And I must say, it was even more amazing than I imagined it would be."

"Like I said, it can't happen again," she huffed. "Otherwise, I'm going to have to put someone else on this assignment."

Now she had his attention. With two long strides, he stood before her and gently grabbed her chin, forcing her to meet his gaze.

"We have an agreement." He leaned in close, but stopped just before his lips touched hers. "And if I wanted someone else to guard me, I would have hired someone else. I want you. Besides, sweetheart, we signed a contract. You're mine for two months."

Dear Reader,

Trinity Layton has recently launched her own personal security agency. It's a good thing, too, since her brother's best friend, Gunner Brooks, is in need of a bodyguard. After once having a crush on Gunner, Trinity thinks she's immune to the sinfully sexy poker player, but he tempts her in ways she's not prepared for.

Gunner can admit to being a skirt chaser back in his college days, but now he's no longer the self-centered, egotistical womanizer Trinity once thought him to be. He plans to show her the man he has become. But there are two things Trinity Layton can't stand: gamblers and liars. And what she remembers of Gunner is that he's both.

So go ahead. Dive into *Sin City Temptation*. But I must warn you, be prepared for a fun ride of passion, suspense and steamy sex scenes!

Enjoy!

Sharon C. Cooper

SharonCooper.net

Sin City
TEMPTATION

SHARON C. COOPER

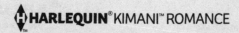
HARLEQUIN® KIMANI™ ROMANCE

Recycling programs
for this product may
not exist in your area.

ISBN-13: 978-0-373-86396-9

Sin City Temptation

Printed in U.S.A.

Sharon C. Cooper spent ten years as a sheet metal worker before becoming a bestselling author. While enjoying that line of work, she earned her BA from Concordia University in business management with an emphasis in communication. When Sharon is not writing or working, she's hanging out with her amazing husband, doing volunteer work or reading a good book (a romance, of course). To read more about Sharon and her novels, visit sharoncooper.net.

Books by Sharon C. Cooper

Harlequin Kimani Romance

Legal Seduction
Sin City Temptation

Visit the Author Profile page at
Harlequin.com for more titles.

To the hero in my life, AL. Thank you for your ongoing support and encouragement. I can't imagine doing all that I do without you in my corner! I love you more than words could ever express!

Acknowledgments

Many thanks to the readers who support my work and make me want to continue writing passionate stories!

Chapter 1

"I still can't believe he stole my money."

Trinity Layton paced the length of her office. Anger bounced inside her gut each time she thought about how her business manager had somehow stolen thousands from her. What made the situation even worse—if she hadn't heard from the IRS claiming her taxes were delinquent, there was no telling when she would have realized something was amiss.

"When was the last time you talked to Ryan?" her brother, Maxwell, asked as he lounged on the sofa on the other side of her office, flipping through a magazine.

"Two weeks ago." She dropped down in her desk chair and folded her arms across her chest. "I tried calling him yesterday after getting off the telephone with the IRS. The first few times I called, I got his voice mail. A few hours later, his phone was disconnected.

So I dropped by his office. The only things I found were late notices and dust bunnies floating across the floor. It's like he's vanished."

"That's messed up."

"Yeah, and he better hope the cops catch him before I do," Trinity mumbled. "He hasn't filed our taxes for the last two quarters. Can you believe that mess?"

She swiveled her chair around to stare out of the large window behind her desk. She had started Layton's Executive Protection Agency, LEPA, nine months ago, using the money from a settlement she had won against the Los Angeles Police Department. After nine years on the police force, when a lieutenant post became available, she applied for the position. Despite being more than qualified, she'd been told that she was too young and inexperienced. Within days, she had filed a discrimination lawsuit.

"So what are you going to do?" Maxwell asked. She turned to face him just as he tossed the magazine onto the table in front of the sofa. "Do you have enough money to take care of the back taxes?"

"Yeah, I'm good, but this nonsense throws off my budget for the next couple of months. Worst case scenario, I'll have to tap into my savings." She could also borrow from the money she'd been setting aside from her own paycheck for the homeless shelter she was looking to open at the end of the year. That would be a last resort.

"Would you have loaned me the money if I needed it?"

"Of course."

She stood and walked across the room and sat on the sofa next to her brother, her champion. The one person always willing and ready to bail her out of any situation. She laid her head on his shoulder and looped her arm through his. "I appreciate you always coming to my rescue."

"That's what big brothers are for." He turned slightly to look at her, forcing her to lift her head. "You seem fairly calm about all of this."

"Don't let my outer calmness fool you. When I see Ryan Coleman, someone is going to have to pull me off of him! I trusted that brotha. I gave him an opportunity to build his business while I build mine, and this is how he repays me. I'm surprised he would do something like this."

"We've known him for years. He wouldn't steal money for no reason, especially from you. He must be in a desperate situation."

"Maybe, but he knew he could have come to me. He was like a brother to me. I'm sure we could've worked something out."

Trinity and Ryan had met when they both were thirteen years old, when he and his parents moved in next door to her family. He was an only child and had spent most of his time hanging out with her and Maxwell.

"So I assume that overall business is good, besides this."

She nodded. "Yeah, business is okay. Of course, it could always be better. I had hoped to have a few more high-end clients by now. Granted, I'm grateful for the repeat customers, but I need things to be steadier. I have to come up with some new ideas to build my business." She knew it was going to take longer than a few months to create the type of clientele list she desired to have one day.

"Anything I can do to help?"

"How about you refer some potential clients my way? Living in Vegas, and being a police sergeant, you must know some people with money who need personal security."

He ran his hand over his mouth in thought, brushing his short beard with his fingers before he stood. "Actually, I do know someone who might be able to benefit from your services."

"What?" She stood and approached him. "You know someone and you haven't said anything before now?"

He slipped into his lightweight jacket.

"The person I'm thinking about just recently mentioned a situation. He might not go for it, but I think he needs a bodyguard."

Trinity didn't miss his hesitation. "Well, who is this person?" She placed her hands on her hips and tilted her head, more curious than ever.

Maxwell leaned against the door to her office. "Gunner Brooks."

Trinity narrowed her eyes at her brother. He knew she couldn't stand his old college roommate and fraternity brother. As a matter of fact, she'd rather eat dirt and drink turpentine than deal with the likes of Gunner Brooks.

She walked back to her desk, shaking her head. "No thanks. I don't know what type of mess Gunner is involved in and I'd just as soon not know. I'm not desperate enough to take him on as a client."

"Hold up." Maxwell pushed away from the door and approached her desk. "A minute ago you wanted to build the business. And what about the homeless shelter? The sooner you get a steady income coming in for the agency, the sooner you can start raising capital for the shelter."

"But—"

"But nothing. I mention a potential client, who is not only wealthy, but also *very* well connected, and you're not interested?"

"Maxwell, you know how I feel about poker and… and gambling, period. After what Daddy put our family through, how can you even suggest I work with Gunner?"

"Trinity, that was a long time ago, and hell, you can't compare Dad with Gunner. Dad was a gambler who relied on luck, never studying how the game is really played."

She couldn't believe what she was hearing and glared at her brother. "How is that any different than what Gunner does?"

"Are you kidding me? There is a huge difference." Maxwell pulled his keys out of his jacket pocket. "Gunner is a professional poker player. He doesn't rely on just luck. To do what he does takes patience, analytical skills, and don't even get me started on the type of self-control a player has to have in order to be any good at the game. Hell, those qualities alone would have ruled Dad out."

He shook his head as if remembering something about Maxwell Layton, Sr. "Dad was an out-of-control gambler who would let losing twenty bucks send him on a drinking binge, whereas Gunner treats playing poker like a job, understanding you win some, you lose some. Unlike a person who has a gambling problem, Gunner is always studying the game, learning his opponents' playing styles, and more than that, Trinity, he takes what he does very seriously."

Trinity rolled her eyes and sat at her desk. "If you say so, but from what I can tell, it's all the same. He's a gambler."

Trinity would never forget the number of times she had heard her parents arguing about how her father spent the grocery or bill money at the casinos. How many times had she wondered what type of man would gamble away the household funds, not caring whether or not his family had a roof over their heads or food on the table?

"Listen, Trinity, try not to compare Gunner to Dad. Gunner has made an amazing living doing something he has trained for, spending his days and nights studying the game. Dad was a wannabe and unfortunately he didn't have what it took to be that type of poker player."

Trinity fought back the anger that surfaced. "And it was at our expense. He left us." She gripped the arms of her chair in order to control the rage brewing in her gut. "He left Momma broke with two kids, not caring whether we lived or died. For that, I will never forgive him."

"Well, you need to try." Maxwell bent down and kissed the top of her head. "He's been dead for years. You need to figure out a way to forgive him so that you can move on and not hold on to all the anger built up inside you. It's not healthy."

Forgiving her father was easier said than done. It was because of him that they had moved to Los Angeles from Vegas with nothing. If it weren't for her mother's family taking them in and helping her find a job, they would have had to continue living in a shelter.

Trinity dropped her shoulders, knowing that her brother was right, but unable to wrap her mind around the idea of working with Gunner or being anywhere near him, for that matter.

"I don't think you're in any position to turn down potential clients. Besides, just because you have issues with Gunner, doesn't mean you can't provide him with a top-notch bodyguard and take care of those back taxes. Unless, of course, you'd prefer to draw money from your savings."

Trinity rocked in her seat. She really couldn't afford to turn down work. Maxwell was right. It was not like she had to hang out with Gunner for any long period of time. All she had to do was find out what his needs were and then connect him with one of her more than qualified security specialists. And if he was still the notorious playboy that she remembered, she was sure he'd be more than excited to have one of her supermodel-look-alikes as a bodyguard.

With a renewed energy, she rubbed her hands together, excited about the possibility of getting a wealthy new client. "Okay, give him my number."

"Trinity?"

Trinity glanced up from the computer. Connie, her assistant and best friend, hurried into the office and closed the door. She stepped to Trinity's desk, her hand pressed against her chest and a dreamy expression on her face.

"Oh, my God," she breathed. "The sexiest human being that ever walked the face of the earth is standing at my desk and he's asking for you."

"Oh," Trinity said nonchalantly and waved her off good-naturedly. "That's probably Gunner Brooks."

"I knew he was nice-looking, but dang! The internet didn't do him justice. That man is downright *fine!*"

"Yeah, yeah, yeah, just send him in." Days after her conversation with Maxwell, Gunner had called and set up an appointment to meet with her.

Trinity went back to typing the letter she was working on, not surprised by the effect Gunner had on Connie. She had witnessed the same reaction plenty of times when visiting Max on the University of Southern California campus when he and Gunner roomed together. Girls were always fawning over Gunner, willing to do anything he asked of them. Funny thing was, he didn't have to say or do much to attract them. There was something about him. Some type of allure that caused women to stop and take notice. Trinity never could put her finger on what it really was that warranted that type of reaction. Thankfully, she was immune to his charming ways.

Moments later a shiver ran up and down her arms and the intoxicating scent of sandalwood and vanilla filled the space. She didn't have to look up to know that Gunner had stepped into her office.

Trinity slowly swiveled in her chair and came face to face with the man who had starred in many of her dreams. She stood as Gunner decreased the distance between them and quickly realized that she wasn't as immune to him as she had thought. Smooth skin the color of rich dark chocolate and a gaze that burrowed into her flesh made her temporarily forget that she couldn't stand him. He flashed his million-dollar smile and everything within her turned to mush. It didn't help that he had his baseball cap pulled low over his eyes, making him look sexy as hell. She always did have a weakness for men wearing baseball caps.

Crap. This might not be as easy as I thought.

She swiped sweaty palms down the sides of her black slacks and stepped from around the desk. She didn't want to be attracted to a man who could easily talk a woman out of her panties and into his bed with only a few words.

"Trinity." His deep voice washed over her like liquid fire, sending heat to every nerve ending in her body. He definitely hadn't lost the swagger that had made him one of the most popular men at USC. His easy, confident gait carried him the short distance across the room and he stopped in front of her. "It's been a long time."

She blew out a breath and straightened her back, refusing to let his nearness unnerve her. Extending her hand, she planned to keep the meeting as professional as possible. Yet instead of shaking her hand, Gunner grabbed hold of her and pulled her into his arms. The contact sent a heated jolt of awareness through her body and she trembled involuntarily.

"We're way past handshakes," he mumbled near her ear and placed a lingering kiss on her cheek. Her eyes drifted closed, hypnotized by the caress of his lips and the heady scent of his cologne. He took a half step back, still not releasing her, and held her at arm's length. "You have grown into a beautiful woman."

His last comment broke the trance and Trinity gracefully shook out of his grip. She walked back around her desk, needing to put some distance between them.

"Excuse me," Connie said, standing near the door. "May I get either one of you a cup of coffee or maybe some ice water?" She looked pointedly at Trinity, humor in her eyes.

Trinity hadn't noticed her standing there, and ignored the knowing look Connie gave her. "Nothing for me, thanks." She turned her attention to her guest. "What about you, Gunner?"

"Actually, coffee would be great."

"Cream, sugar?" Connie asked sweetly.

"Black would be perfect. Thanks, sweetheart." Gunner winked and returned his attention to Trinity, who had to keep herself from rolling her eyes at Connie's departing giggle.

"It's good to see you again, Gunner." Trinity hoped her words sounded more sincere than she felt. He might have been one of the *finest* men she'd ever met, but he was still someone she wanted nothing to do with. "I'm glad you were able to stop by. Please have a seat."

He removed the ratty baseball cap that had a gold omega symbol across the front, and sat in one of the leather armchairs facing her desk. Ruggedly handsome, Gunner exuded self-confidence, making it hard for Trinity not to stare at him. Every move he made her gaze seemed to follow. It wasn't until he crossed an ankle over his knee and his eyes met hers that she realized she was entranced.

He smiled. Heat rose to her cheeks and she diverted her eyes to the file that she'd been working on earlier. It was time to get it together and tap into her professional demeanor. Breathing in and out slowly, without making it seem too obvious, she felt herself relax...some. Placing the file off to the side, she grabbed her notepad.

"Okay, let's get started." She scribbled the date and

time on the pad of paper before she returned her attention to him.

"Why don't we catch up first?" Gunner said and slouched a little in his seat, appearing cool and relaxed.

No one would ever believe he was wealthy by his posture or by the way he was dressed. A gold T-shirt that read I Always Wear My Poker Face, stretched across his taut muscles and hugged his large biceps. With well-worn jeans and a pair of scuffed wheat-colored Timberland boots, he looked more like a thug than the multimillionaire that she had researched.

"Excuse me," Connie said.

Seeing the coffee in her hand, Trinity waved her in. Connie placed the steaming liquid in front of Gunner and a bottle of water with a cup of ice in front of Trinity before closing the door behind her.

"I haven't seen you in years. I was surprised when Max told me that you had left LAPD and started your own personal protection business. I'm impressed." He fingered a stunning gold bracelet on his wrist that had writing on it, which she couldn't make out, but was outlined with diamonds. She glanced up to find him studying her.

Trinity sat back in her seat and took another deep breath before speaking. "Thanks. It's been my lifelong dream to have my own business. After serving on the police force for nine years, it seemed to be a logical business to go into."

"You must be a serious bad-ass. I heard you worked SWAT the last two years you were with LAPD."

Trinity twirled her ink pen between her fingers. Apparently, she wasn't bad-ass enough, seeing that she'd gotten snubbed for the lieutenant position. It was the second time she hadn't been seriously considered for a position that she was more than qualified to hold. Her superior had often made comments about her still being wet behind the ears, and how women were created to stay home and have babies.

Her gripped tightened on her pen. She'd had plenty of time to let the bad feelings she had for LAPD pass. Yet, every now and then animosity of how she had been treated snuck in.

"Hey," Gunner sat forward, "didn't mean to bring up any bad memories. Are you all right? It looked as if I lost you for a moment there."

Trinity gave herself a mental shake. "Oh, yeah, I'm fine. Being on the force and then getting the SWAT assignment prepared me for all of this," she said, raising her hands and glancing around her office. "No regrets."

He regarded her spacious office as he nodded. "Nice digs you have here." Trinity followed his gaze, proud of what she had accomplished. The location of her office building was costing her a pretty penny, but it was worth it to be in a prime area. "So how long have you been in business?" Gunner asked. "Tell me a little about your agency."

She rocked a little in her leather office chair, finally feeling comfortable with having him in her space. "I opened the agency about nine months ago and so far things are going well. I started with five security specialists on call. Now I have twenty that I use on a regular basis. All are very well trained and either have a police or military background, as well as expertise in various areas of personal security." She stopped rocking and slid forward in her seat. "So I have no doubt that I have someone who can meet your needs. Why don't you tell me why you need a bodyguard?"

Gunner sat back in his seat, still finding it hard to believe that little Trinity Layton was all grown up. Thanks to her brother, Maxwell, he had kept up with her career, the good and the not-so-good aspects. But what Maxwell failed to mention was how *fine* his sister was. Flawless skin the color of coffee with a hint of cream. Her brown hair that hung just past her shoulders was longer than he remembered, with copper highlights that brought out the gold specks in her light brown eyes. She was cute back when she'd visited them at USC, but now she was downright gorgeous. He'd bet that whenever she arrested anyone, they went willingly in order to be close to her.

Gunner had originally shot down the idea of hiring a bodyguard when Maxwell first suggested it, since he could take care of himself. Yet, he reconsidered when Max explained that Trinity was trying to build the agency's clientele. Now, after seeing her again, he was glad he'd flown to LA to meet with her.

"In the last couple of weeks, a few professional poker players who are gearing up for the PPO, the Poker Play-Offs, have been involved in a few incidents."

"What type of incidents?" Trinity asked.

For the first time since he arrived, she seemed relaxed and genuinely interested in what he had to say. When he had first walked into her office, she appeared to be about ready to bolt for the door. Her expression reminded him of the first time he'd met her. They both seemed to be shocked into speechlessness. Gunner couldn't believe Maxwell had a cutie-pie sister, but he wasn't sure what her thoughts had been. All he knew was there was a sweet shyness about her mixed with a little I-don't-take-crap-from-anyone. He had been attracted to her back when he was in college, but never made a move on her. Not because she happened to be Max's little sister, but because Trinity was serious-girlfriend material, and back then he was all about having a good time without the commitment.

Now that Gunner was thinking more and more about settling down and having a family, he was viewing commitment and relationships differently. He no longer dated just to be dating. Instead, he only spent time with women whom he was attracted to and could see building a future with. Needless to say, the list was short. Most women only saw him as their ticket to financial freedom. He knew enough about Trinity to know that she was the type of woman he was looking to settle down with—independent, had good values and came from a good family. The fact that she was absolutely gorgeous didn't hurt either.

Gunner toyed with the PPO diamond bracelet that he had won the previous year, the fifth of his collection. "A participant was jumped shortly after leaving a tournament," he finally answered. "Another walked into a grocery store and was stabbed in the side by an unknown assailant, the knife barely missing some major organs. And just recently, one of the tournament participants left a popular restaurant and was hit in the head with a steel rod. The attacker got away."

"Those incidents sound like something that could happen to anyone, especially someone who hangs out at a casino, gambling away hard-earned cash. I'd think that would be an everyday occurrence in Vegas." The distaste with which Trinity said the words didn't go unnoticed by Gunner. He had a feeling she didn't like him, but the disgust he heard in her tone sounded like something else was going on.

"This has caught some of the players' attention because none of the individuals in these instances were robbed. Only roughed up or injured to the point of having to drop out of the tournament. Also, each occurrence happened away from the casinos. *And* most important, the victims were favorites to earn one of nine spots at the PPO's Main Event." When it looked as if she didn't understand how huge that was, he continued. "The PPO is to poker what the Super Bowl is to football. Each year, individuals compete for a seat at the final table. Three of the nine people favored for this year are out of commission and unable to compete."

Understanding showed in Trinity's eyes and she stopped twirling the pen in her hand. "I assume you're one of the favorites?"

Gunner met her gaze and nodded. "I am. Assuming someone doesn't take me out first."

Silence fell between Trinity and Gunner. She had recently read about the PPO, not fully understanding how it worked. What she did remember though, was that the fee to enter the tournament was over ten thousand dollars with a multimillion-dollar cash prize. She had also learned that Gunner had participated in the PPO every year since he was twenty-one and had won the main event five times. Despite his laid-back attitude and disinterested demeanor, Gunner Brooks was worth an obscene amount of money.

Trinity stood and unplugged her laptop. "Let's go over to the round table so that I can show you what I'm working with." When she glanced up to find him with an amused expression on his face, she realized what she'd said. "Uh, I mean so that I can show you the security specialists that you can choose from."

He followed her to the table and waited until she sat before he took the chair next to hers. Trinity quickly realized that suggesting they move to the table might not have been a good idea. Not only did he smell divine, if he sat any closer to her, they could share the same seat.

Moving her chair over without making it too obvious, she hurried and pulled up the computer file that contained portfolios of all of her bodyguards.

"All of our security specialists are highly qualified." She glanced at him before returning her attention back to the computer. "Would you prefer a male or a female bodyguard?"

"Female," he said simply. He'd always been a man of few words and Trinity wasn't surprised that he would want a woman protecting him. Men like him typically chose a woman, not wanting people around them knowing they had a bodyguard.

"How long will you need our security specialist?"

"I want someone who is available 24/7 for the next two, two-and-a-half, months. They'll need to be willing to travel to tournaments, as well as other events during the PPO."

Trinity mentally calculated the amount of money she would make with this contract and did a happy dance in her head. With the payment plan she had in place for her clients, the down payment alone would more than cover the back taxes. She'd also be able to save some money. She was going to owe her brother big for referring Gunner.

Trinity opened the computer file and the faces of ten women of varied nationalities appeared on the screen. Gunner stirred next to her, but he said nothing.

"Okay, let's start with Diamond. She's a certified stunt woman and a martial arts instructor who works at one of the dojos here in town. She's available for the assignment and has no problem with spending a couple of months traveling to tournaments with you."

Trinity went through all of the women's profiles, but was pretty sure Gunner would pick Willow. She looked like a beauty queen and had a degree in finance, but most important, she was a weapons specialist with a black belt in tae kwon do. Any man of his caliber would love to have a woman like her by his side.

When Gunner clicked through the choices again and arrived at the end without responding, she wondered if she might have misunderstood exactly what he was looking for.

"If you would prefer someone different or have changed your mind and would rather go with a male bodyguard, that can easily be arranged." She turned the laptop slightly toward her and started to pull up a different set of specialists, but Gunner placed his hand over hers, halting her fingers on the keyboard.

Trinity's heart lurched in her chest and she stared down at his large hand that covered hers. Heat from his touch soared though her body. She couldn't end this meeting fast enough.

She eased her hand from beneath his and placed it in her lap as Gunner said, "You don't have to show me anymore. I've decided."

Chapter 2

Gunner pushed back from the table and stretched out his legs. Scratching his head, he kept his gaze on the computer screen. He had taken an early commuter flight to meet with Trinity this morning, hoping to set everything in place before flying back to Vegas for a tournament that evening. But right now, he was so exhausted and attracted to Trinity, he could barely think straight.

He twisted his upper body from side to side, trying to work out a few kinks in his back before he leaned back and stretched his arms above his head. Resettling in his seat, he lifted the tepid cup of coffee to his lips and glanced at Trinity over the rim of the cup. He couldn't get over how gorgeous she was. A Gabrielle Union lookalike, he had no doubt that she turned heads wherever she went. He zeroed in on her left hand, checking her ring finger. Max had never mentioned her being in a serious relationship or being married, but that didn't mean she wasn't. And if she wasn't, he wondered why not. A woman like her would be a welcomed addition to any man's life. Who knows, maybe even his life.

"Okay, so who's it going to be?" Trinity folded her hands on top of the table. "I assume you saw someone you like?"

A slow smile spread across Gunner's lips. *I definitely see something I like. Only it isn't on the computer screen.* "Where did you find these women? Their skills and accomplishments are very impressive and they look as if they should be strutting their stuff on some runway, modeling the latest fashions. You have an awesome team."

Trinity smiled, which was something she hadn't done much of since he had arrived. Her whole face lit up and he liked it.

"Thank you. It wasn't easy finding them," she said. "I wanted to recruit people who could easily blend in with my clientele. The women I have just shown you are refined, but won't have a problem kicking someone's butt if necessary."

Gunner nodded, his gaze steady on Trinity. The longer he stared at her, the more he could sense her cool, calm demeanor slipping. She was trying to be professional, but he'd known years ago that there was a mutual attraction between the two of them. And he had every intention of confirming that the attraction was now stronger than ever.

She scooted back in her seat and her fresh lavender scent sailed into his space. Never one for holding back on going after what he wanted, he nevertheless resisted the urge to touch her since it seemed to make her uncomfortable. Enchanting eyes, a smile that could light up the darkest room, and a do-me-baby body that had him adjusting himself every few minutes. Oh, yeah, he definitely wanted her. He could still remember how it felt when he found out she was Max's baby sister. It was like having ice-cold water dumped on his head. He couldn't believe that this Nubian princess, this love-at-first-sight woman, was related to his roomie. He'd made the right decision in not pursuing her all those years ago, but now all bets were off. She was all grown up and he planned to get to know the woman she had become.

"So?" Trinity's voice invaded his musings. She crossed her long leg over the opposite knee, her high-heel-clad foot swinging back and forth. "Which one is it going to be?"

Gunner sucked in a breath and released it slowly. He placed his lucky baseball cap on his head and pulled it low over his eyes before he turned his attention to her.

"None of them." He stood.

"What?" She leaped up. "What do you mean none of them? Those women are the best security specialists in the business. You will never find one more capable than any one of them."

Gunner nodded, loving the way her light brown eyes grew darker the madder she got. "I believe you, but there is one female bodyguard who's on your staff whose profile you didn't show me."

Trinity put her hands on her hips. Her expression indicated that she was thoroughly confused. "Who? I showed you everyone."

Gunner shook his head and picked up his almost empty coffee cup. "Nope. Not everyone."

Anxiety stirred in Trinity's gut. She couldn't afford to lose this contract.

"Well, let me show you some other choices. I'm sure we have someone who will fit your needs," she said.

"I told you. That won't be necessary. I already know who I want."

Trinity's patience was slowly being overshadowed by her anger. Gunner might've played games for a living, but she didn't like games. If he was playing her... She shook her head, not completing the thought. *Okay, think, Trinity, think.* There had to be a way to save this contract. *Who did I miss?* She searched her mind, mentally going through her list of female security specialists, and came up empty. She couldn't think of anyone she had missed.

"Gunner, I'm sorry, but unless you have a name of the person you're thinking about, I can't help you. Won't you reconsider one of the individuals that I've shown you?" She had never begged anyone for anything, but thinking about the amount of money at stake and her financial situation, she wouldn't be too proud to beg right now.

He approached her, his lazy gait intensifying his sex appeal. This man was a danger to any woman's peace of mind. For every step forward he took, she took an unconscious step back until the heel of her foot hit the wall and there was nowhere to go. He didn't stop until he stood before her, totally invading her personal space. Trinity couldn't step away even if she wanted to and at the moment she wasn't sure she did. His dark, sexy eyes, slightly shielded by the brim of his cap, held her captive. *So much for being immune to his good looks and charming ways.*

She swallowed hard, trying not to lean in and capture his tempting lips. *I will not give in to temptation. I will not give in to temptation,* she chanted over and over in her head. But her defenses were weakening. *Okay, think, Trinity. Think.*

"Uh, is it someone from a different agency?" she finally asked. "Because if it is, I'm hoping you'll give me a chance to change your mind."

Gunner shook his head. "Oh, no, I'm going with your agency. It's just that you didn't show me the bodyguard that I have in mind." The back of his hand slid down her cheek and an erotic jolt shook everything within her. It took all she had not to lean into his touch. "There is only one person on your team that I would consider having my back for the next couple of months."

"Who?" she asked just above a whisper, her gaze meeting his.

Seconds ticked by before he spoke. "You."

She tilted her head, totally shocked by his response. "Me?"

The right corner of his mouth lifted into a sexy grin. "Yeah. You."

He pushed a lock of her hair behind her ear, and Trinity held her breath until he dropped his arm. Of all the things he could have said, the last thing she expected was for him to request her.

She blew out a quick breath and stepped around him. "Gunner, I'm flattered, but I...I'm not available," she stuttered, floored that he would request her to guard him. "I've shown you plenty of women who are more than capable of handling this assignment. We can go through the choices again. I'm sure any of them will exceed your expectations."

"Why aren't you available?" Once again, for each step he took toward her, she took two steps back. It was as if they were creating their own dance moves. "Are you married? Kids?"

She shook her head. "No. No, nothing like that. It's just that I have to be here to run my business. I can't afford to take an assignment for that long."

"What if I paid you double your rate?" He finally stopped moving toward her.

Trinity took a moment to catch her breath. His closeness had her all worked up, which was uncharacteristic for her. She had stared down hardened criminals and dealt with out-of-control drug addicts on a daily basis for years. Yet there was something about Gunner that made everything within her jumble together.

She shook herself and mentally calculated what the amount would be if he doubled her rate. She would be crazy to turn down that kind of money. But she also knew that she'd never be able to handle being in his presence 24/7. Despite what she told herself, she was *not* immune to Gunner Brooks. The attraction she felt for him was stronger than ever.

"Well?" Gunner prodded. "Do we have a deal?"

Trinity shook her head. "Gunner—"

"What if I tripled your fee? Then would we have a deal?" he asked, his voice an octave lower.

Trinity's breath caught in her throat. She knew he

was wealthy and could easily afford her rates, but triple? Her mother hadn't raised a fool.

"When would you like for me to start?"

Chapter 3

"I can't believe you're moving in with a man."

Trinity rolled her eyes at Connie, ignoring her friend's comment and laughter. In all honesty, Trinity couldn't believe she'd be temporarily moving in with Gunner either. The whole situation felt like an out-of-body experience. What were the chances she'd be living under the same roof as the person she'd had a crush on years ago? On the other hand, this would give her an opportunity to understand what several of her security specialists dealt with when a client hired a twenty-four-hour guard. So far, she wasn't looking forward to spending so much time with Gunner.

"I don't know why you're making such a big deal about all of this," Connie said, standing in the doorway of Trinity's walk-in closet. "Do you know how many women would kill for this opportunity? Not only is the man wealthy, but he's also gorgeous. If I had the skills to be one of your security specialists, heck, I'd be in his face explaining to him why I was the better choice."

Trinity shook her head and smiled. Connie Shaw, her best friend since high school, was five-four and a hundred and ten pounds soaking wet. Trinity couldn't ask for a better assistant, but knew her friend could barely fight off a fly, let alone some unknown enemy.

Trinity didn't know if Gunner's concerns regarding someone taking out professional poker players were warranted, but she had every intention of protecting her new client. She was an expert in her line of business, and she didn't plan on allowing her personal feelings to get in the way of her doing her job.

"Since Vegas will probably be a thousand degrees this time a year, I'm thinking you're going to need these."

Trinity looked up to see a canary yellow, two-piece bathing suit dangling from Connie's fingers, a wicked grin spread across her friend's mouth. Trinity might take a swimsuit, but it would definitely not be that particular one. The scrap of material barely covered her most prized possessions.

"Connie, you can put those items back where you found them. This is not a pleasure trip." Trinity went back to packing. She grabbed her toiletries from the bathroom and stuffed them in her carry-on suitcase.

"I know it won't be professional for you to have any fun on this trip with the hunk."

"His name is Gunner."

"Okay, then I know it won't be any fun on this trip with Gunner, the hunk, but what if it—"

"It won't."

"Or what if he—"

"He won't."

Connie threw the rolled-up pair of socks that she had in her hand at Trinity, who caught it before it made contact with her head.

"Stop that and let me finish my sentence!"

"Violent, are we?" Trinity teased.

"If you keep up this attitude, you're going to end up an old maid who lives with nine cats," Connie said and disappeared into the closet, but soon returned with a pair of red do-me-baby stilettos. "You never know when love might find you, but at this rate and with this negative attitude of yours, you're going to miss it!"

Trinity continued packing, adding the shoes that Connie put near the bed to one of the larger suitcases sitting on the floor. She tuned Connie out as she went on her usual rant regarding Trinity's love life, or lack thereof. Ever since Connie started dating Todd, a guy from her cooking class, she'd been pointing out the fact that Trinity wasn't seeing anyone and hadn't had a date in months.

As far as Trinity was concerned, getting her business to turn a profit was her main goal. Besides, right now, she didn't have anything to offer anyone. She had too many balls in the air and she refused to let any of them fall by taking her eyes off her aspirations. This time next year, she wanted LEPA to have a solid list of clients and she wanted her homeless shelter up and running. Every aspect of her life was wrapped up into those two objectives.

"It's getting late. Are you still planning to visit your homeless friends, or should I say your *peeps*, this evening?" Connie asked.

Trinity glanced at her Michael Kors watch, last

year's birthday present to herself. Connie was right—
if she didn't leave soon, it would be dark before she
made it to the outskirts of Skid Row, a heavy popu-
lated area where the homeless resided in downtown
Los Angeles.

"I'm glad you said something." Trinity placed a few
more items in the suitcase. She grabbed the bag of
clothes that was set aside for Lucy, a homeless woman
that Trinity went to see a couple of times a month. "I
still think you should go with me. I might need you to
check on Lucy, Fred and Henry while I'm gone."

Connie, who was sitting on the bed near the suitcase, looked at her as if she had lost her mind. "You
know I can't handle being around homeless people. If
that makes me a horrible person, I'm sorry, but unlike
you, I can't stomach the area where they live or the
condition in which they live."

Trinity moved the suitcase and sat next to her friend
as she slipped into her tennis shoes. "It doesn't make
you a bad person. I remember when my mom moved
Maxwell and me from Vegas to Los Angeles. We were
homeless, living out of her raggedy car that barely got
us to LA, and eating one meal a day until some of her
relatives took us in."

Trinity would never forget hearing her mother's
sobs fill the interior of the car when she thought that
she and Maxwell were asleep. Even as a child, Trinity
had started planning for the homeless shelter that she
would one day open.

"As a cop, I remember the first time I worked the
area. I was a mess. My heart broke for each and every
homeless person I came in contact with. I just wanted
to take them home with me or find suitable housing for

all of them." Trinity adjusted her pant legs and stood. "That's why I have to get this homeless shelter up and running. Every night when I curl up in my warm bed or eat a hot meal, I think of them. We live in one of the richest countries in the world. As far as I'm concerned, there is no excuse for anyone to be homeless."

"But I thought you said that many of them prefer to stay where they are, that they're choosing to be homeless."

"Yeah, but not all of them." Trinity would never forget the time that she had found an opening at a woman's shelter for Lucy. The woman had refused to go, claiming it was unsafe and that people would steal her stuff.

"That's unbelievable. I can't imagine choosing the streets over a warm bed."

Trinity stood near the dresser, looking into the mirror. She pulled a lightweight sweatshirt over her head and exchanged her expensive watch for the one that she used when working in the yard.

"I want to have a place available to those who've fallen on hard times and *do* want to get off the streets."

"And if anyone can do it, I know you can." Connie slid off the bed and grabbed her large handbag from the chair near the window. "Is Jesse able to check on your peeps while you're away?"

Trinity nodded with a hair clip between her teeth. She pulled back her hair and put it into a ponytail. Jesse was one of her old partners at the LAPD, a good friend, who often worked the area near Skid Row.

"Yeah, he said he'll keep an eye on them while I'm away."

"Okay, but in the meantime, you be careful down there."

Trinity turned off the bedroom light and followed Connie out of the room and down the short hallway to the small living room area of her Hollywood Hills condominium. Trinity didn't know what to expect with regard to where she'd be living when she went to Vegas, but she was definitely going to miss her cheery condo. During her time on the police force, most days she couldn't wait to get home. She looked forward to her walls painted with bright colors, her large bay window that let in lots of sunlight, and most important, she loved the cozy environment that she had created. The intimate space kept her grounded...and sane.

"Do you still want me to pick you up at six in the morning?" Connie asked, standing at the door, her hand on the doorknob.

"Definitely, that should give me plenty of time to get to the airport and check my bags."

"All right then, I'll see you in the morning. Be safe out there."

Forty-five minutes later, Trinity found a parking spot near San Pedro Street. She did a once-over of her attire, ensuring that she had remembered to leave anything of value at home. Most times when she visited, she didn't have any problems, but every now and then some fool approached her thinking that she was an easy target. Just in case, she had a small handgun in her ankle holster and a Swiss Army Knife shoved down into the pocket of her jeans.

She climbed out of the car and grabbed the supplies that she had specifically brought for Lucy, Fred and Henry. Since the day they helped her catch a man who had robbed several Dollar Stores and killed two people, she had adopted them as family.

Trinity discretely put her finger under her nose. She didn't think she'd ever get used to the smell of garbage and funk as she walked the short block to where her peeps hung out. Trash littered the area. A suffocating sensation tightened her throat as she wandered deeper into the throes of homeless people, noticing there were more of them than the last time she was there. Trinity stepped around a man who was stretched across the sidewalk, facedown, and prayed that he was alive. With the poor conditions, lack of food and nonexistent health care for them, it wasn't uncommon for some to die right there on the street.

She spotted Fred and Henry first, wondering why Lucy wasn't with them. It wasn't until she got closer that she noticed someone lying on cardboard behind the makeshift card table they had set up.

"Well, if it isn't our favorite cop," Fred said, tossing the cards that were in his hands to the table and telling Henry to deal. They all knew she was no longer a cop, but still referred to her as one. "I was just thinking that it was about time we saw you."

"I know. I was hoping to get here last week, but things have been a little busy." She handed each of them a bag of toiletries, as well as some food. She set Lucy's bags next to her shopping cart, which was sitting near her head and was spilling over with junk. Trinity glanced down at Lucy's sleeping form. "How's she been doing?"

The last time Trinity visited, Lucy was having hip trouble and could barely walk, but refused to seek medical attention.

"About the same," Henry said. "She's been sleeping a lot more, but says she's fine."

"Lucy," Fred called out trying to wake her without taking his eyes off the recently dealt cards in his hands. "Trinity's here to see you." Fred winked at Trinity and she rewarded him with a smile.

Lucy removed the blanket that had been covering most of her face and head, but didn't sit up. Trinity didn't miss the dark circles beneath her eyes or how pale her café au lait complexion looked.

"What's going on, Luce?" Trinity asked. She eased behind Fred's crate and knelt down near her friend, feeling her forehead and then checking her pulse, which seemed a little fast. "Are you feeling okay?" Trinity helped her sit up, pushing the knit cap Lucy was wearing farther away from her face so that she could get a better look at her eyes.

Lucy swatted Trinity's hand away. "Stop that. I feel fine. Besides, I told you to quit all that fussing over me. We're going to have to find you a man so you can get married, have some babies and fuss over them."

Trinity shook her head and smiled. She had to endure the marriage speech in various forms during every visit. Like many women, Trinity dreamed of the day she'd fall in love, get married and start a family, but she didn't see the fantasy coming to fruition anytime soon.

Trinity studied her friend and concern welled up in her heart at how bad Lucy looked. Her health was clearly declining and Trinity would never forgive herself if she didn't do everything she could for Lucy.

Just another reason why I need to get that shelter up and running.

Pulling out one of the bottled waters she'd brought, Trinity opened it and handed the bottle to Lucy, insisting that she drink from it. Lucy had once been married.

Years ago, she had been a housekeeper for a wealthy family and enjoyed the work until she was accused of stealing. Anger bubbled inside Trinity every time she thought about the bad hand Lucy had been dealt. Instead of taking her word and basing their decision on Lucy's commitment to their family, her employer terminated her without proving whether or not she'd stolen anything. Then, after a long period of unemployment, her husband eventually left her, taking the kids with him. That was twenty-some years ago and Lucy never forgave herself for not fighting to keep her children. Now they were grown, with kids of their own, and wanted a relationship with Lucy, but she refused. According to her, she didn't want to be a burden to them, and nothing Trinity did or said could convince Lucy otherwise.

Trinity dug through the bag of food that she'd brought and pulled out a protein bar. "Why don't you try eating something? I can tell you've lost some weight—making me even more concerned."

Lucy pushed the bar away. "I told you that I was fine. Why don't you pick on Fred or Henry?"

Right now Trinity's main concern was getting Lucy some medical attention, but she had no idea how. She was leaving for Vegas in the morning and unless she was able to convince Lucy to go to the hospital at that moment, there was no telling when her friend would get some help.

Lucy looked away when her eyes met Trinity's concerned ones. "I'm worried about you," Trinity said in a low voice. "I can't leave town knowing that you're not well."

"Trinity," Lucy said in that tone that mothers, no

matter the nationality, use to get their child's attention. "I told you I was fine. Now give it a rest!"

"Luce, let me take you to the hospital." Trinity ignored Lucy's growing agitation. "I'm heading out of town in the morning, and I won't be able to focus on what I'm supposed to do if—"

"She ain't gonna go," Henry said. He adjusted his broken glasses, held together by duct tape, and looked over their rims at Trinity huddled next to Lucy. Trinity should've known Henry was listening, considering his hearing was sharp, unlike his poor eyesight. "We tried to get her to go up there to that clinic a few blocks over," he pointed behind them, "but she wouldn't hear of it."

"Henry, mind your own business." Lucy glared at him as she repositioned herself against the brick building. "I've been taking care of myself for over fifty years. I don't need you—" she turned to Trinity "—or *you* telling me what to do. Besides, shouldn't you be home packing or something? And what is this trip? Where are you off to?"

Trinity sighed and stood. She glanced at the brick wall behind her, before leaning against it. She'd have Jesse stop by as often as he could to check on Lucy and she'd see if she could get his brother, who was a doctor, to make at least one of those trips with him.

Trinity told them about her pending trip to Vegas and answered their numerous questions. She was going to miss them. They treated her like one of their children and she felt just as close to them as she did her own mother.

"So this fella you're going to be guarding, I assume he's not married?" Lucy perked up.

Trinity shook her head, trying to hide a smile. Lucy didn't quit. "No. He's not married and before you ask, he's not my type."

"He's male and breathing, right?"

"Yes, but…"

Lucy attempted to stand and Trinity, as well as Fred, who was still sitting on a crate, turned slightly and helped her up. "But nothin'. You are a young, beautiful woman. There is only one reason you're still single and that's because you're not giving these young men a chance to get to know you."

"Leave the child alone," Henry chimed in. "She's young. She has plenty of time to settle down."

"It's not her I'm concerned about," Lucy said. Trinity grabbed hold of Lucy's arm and cringed when it looked as if her friend would topple over. Lucy waved her off. "I'm concerned that we're not getting any younger and I want her to find that special someone before *we* leave this world."

Chapter 4

The next morning, besides a little small talk, Trinity and Gunner rode in silence. He had picked her up from McCarren International Airport and immediately Trinity was reminded of his net worth. Admiring the interior of Gunner's sleek black Maybach Exelero, the most expensive car ever created, she wondered how many lifetimes it would take her to afford such a luxury vehicle. With its ultra-smooth ride, butter-soft leather seats and impressive dashboard, it had to be one of the sexiest cars she'd ever been in.

Trinity stole a glance at Gunner. *A sexy car for a sexy man.* It amazed her how he could make a simple T-shirt and jeans look sexy as hell. It didn't help that he smelled heavenly, sending all of her senses into overdrive.

"Was your flight all right?" Gunner asked when they were on the highway headed to his house.

"It was fine. Thank you for making all of the arrangements. Riding in first class was nice."

"No problem. It's the least I could do since I'm asking you to leave your home and provide me with around-the-clock service." He winked.

Trinity knew what type of service he was referring to, but she hated how he made it sound. She planned to make sure he knew up front what services she offered…and what she didn't.

Thirty minutes later, they pulled up to a breathtaking house that looked like something straight out of *House & Home*. The sprawling two-story home, flanked with palm trees, shrubs and more windows than Trinity could count, clearly showed the expanse of Gunner's wealth. The house sat back from the street with spectacular mountains as its backdrop.

Gunner pulled into the three-car garage. "So what's it going to take for you to relax around me?" he asked when he turned off the car.

"Who said I'm not relaxed?"

Gunner gave a short laugh that lacked humor and stepped out of the car. He started around the front of the vehicle to open the door for Trinity, but she jumped out before he reached her. She appreciated him being a gentleman, but it was important that he saw her as his security detail. Even though she didn't officially start work until the next day.

"You're kidding, right?" He closed the car door. "As close as you were sitting to the passenger-side door, for a minute I thought you were going to bolt from the car the moment I stopped at a traffic light." Gunner popped open the trunk and removed her bags, lifting them with ease, as if they were empty.

He was right. She had to get herself together and remember that this was a job. He was like any other client. He was just a man. All she had to do was ignore the strong attraction between them. How to do that was the problem. It had been easy when she visited her brother at USC, because, back then, whenever she saw Gunner he was usually hugged-up to some girl. Trinity had thought he was a dog, unworthy of her attraction to him. But now things were different. He seemed more focused, more reserved. She wondered when the transformation had taken place.

"Listen," he said, taking his cap off and running his hand over his short hair, exhaustion covering his features. "Maybe we got off on the wrong foot. I hope you don't feel that I forced you to take the assignment. I honestly think you're the best person for the job. When I'm playing poker, I need to be as focused as possible, no distractions. I didn't think I could do that with someone I wasn't familiar with watching my back. At least with you, though we haven't seen each other in a while, I'm comfortable. Besides, Max said that you're the best and I believe him."

Trinity snorted. "Well, I don't know if you should listen to him. He's kind of biased." She tried lightening the tension. "But I do appreciate you giving me this opportunity. My agency is still fairly new and I need to do whatever I can to make sure it's a success."

Gunner yawned, the third time in the past few minutes. She didn't know what the life of a poker player was like, but she assumed that it included late nights. At least that's how it had been for her father. As a kid, she rarely saw him. In the mornings before she and Maxwell went to school, he'd be sleeping if he was even home. And by the time they returned from school, he'd be gone, gambling away the little money they had.

That thought brought her back to the present. She couldn't stand gamblers. Her father died still trying to strike it rich while hanging out in casinos.

"Why don't I show you around and then you can get settled in?" He yawned. "Ah, man, excuse me." He tilted his head from side to side, as if working out a kink in his neck. "I'm sorry. It's been a long day."

Trinity glanced at her watch. "Uh, it's only nine-thirty in the morning. You must've been awake all night. You didn't have to pick me up. I could have easily gotten a cab."

"Nah, I wanted to. It was the least I could do since I had you dropping everything to take on this assignment."

Trinity waved him off. She couldn't tell him that he had single-handedly saved her agency by writing one fat check. "I'll tell you what. You get some sleep and I'll get settled, then show myself around. Besides, I need to check out your security system, windows and stuff like that."

He shook his head. "I'm not much of a host, but the least I can do is show you around and help you get settled."

"All right—" she shrugged "—suit yourself."

Gunner let them into the house and set her bags inside the mudroom. "I'll come back for these." With his hand on her elbow, a blast of desire shot up her spine and it took everything within her to remain cool. *God help me.* She clearly needed to start dating if a man's touch alone caused her nerves to short circuit.

As they strolled down a short hallway, Trinity eyed

a powder room to the left and several closed sliding doors on the right, which she assumed were closets. Then they stepped into the kitchen.

"I guess there's no need to tell you what room this is."

Trinity glanced around at the high-end granite countertops, custom maple java cabinets, and the top-of-the-line stainless-steel appliances. She ran her hands along the curved breakfast bar, and then stood near one of the high-back black leather bar stools.

"This is definitely a cook's kitchen. Absolutely gorgeous." Cooking was enjoyable in her small two-bedroom, two-bathroom Hollywood Hills condominium, but preparing a meal in his kitchen would be a privilege. "So do you cook?"

Gunner shook his head. "Not a lick. I can't even make toast without burning it." He guided her out of the kitchen area.

The semi-open floor plan provided a clear view of the family room. Off to the left, Trinity noticed another space that would probably be considered a formal dining room if it had a table or even a chandelier. With each step she took, all she could think about was why one person needed so much space.

They moved into the family room and Trinity immediately went to the wall of windows. She stood there for several seconds, gawking at the amazing view of mountains everywhere her gaze landed. Between the kitchen and the view, she could see why Gunner had purchased the home. *Absolutely breathtaking.* She suddenly remembered why she was there. From a security standpoint, the wall-to-wall windows and the lack of window covering presented a security nightmare.

Trinity turned from the windows and looked up. There were even square windows inches below the twenty-foot ceilings. A quick glance around the space revealed either a lack of a security system or one that didn't cover the windows. There was one other thing that struck Trinity as odd—no furniture.

"Did you just move in?" she inquired.

Gunner chuckled. "No, actually I've lived here for two years. I guess it's a little hard to tell, huh?"

"Yeah, a little."

"Maybe while you're here, I can get you to help me pick out some furniture. You're going to soon realize there are a few other rooms that are also vacant of furniture."

Trinity smiled, not surprised by the admission. "You are such a guy." It took her brother Maxwell a couple of years to furnish a couple of rooms in his house as well, and his wasn't half the size of Gunner's.

She continued her walk through the first floor, no longer waiting for Gunner to guide her. After spotting another bathroom, a huge bedroom and a home office, she realized that they were back near the kitchen. Stepping up to the sliding glass doors, she glanced out at the backyard, not surprised to see an enormous pool that took up much of the yard.

"So, do you swim?" Gunner asked.

"Occasionally," she responded when she turned from the glass doors. Gunner stood several feet from her, leaning against a wall in the kitchen, his dark skin creating a perfect contrast next to the stark white backdrop. *Damn, this man is too sexy for his own good.*

Her gaze traveled down his six-foot-one form, his hands stuffed into the pockets of his jeans, his legs crossed at the ankle. She admired how comfortable he seemed in his own skin. He probably had no idea that he looked as if he was posing for the cover of *GQ* magazine. Her gaze eased back up his body and heat rose to her face. Desire rippled through her when she noticed how perfect his jeans outlined the enticing bulge pressing against the front of his pants. *Lord help me.* She had always been attracted to ruggedly handsome men and Gunner was no exception. Everything about him screamed hot sex god. From the five-o'clock shadow lightly covering his strong jaw to his devil-may-care attitude, he was the epitome of sensuality.

She glanced away. *Please God, help me get through these two months without falling under his sensuous spell.* She just had to stay focused on her reason for being there, and not get caught up in the passionate longing that soared through her body whenever she was in his presence.

She returned her attention to him. "I noticed you have an alarm keypad near the front entrance, and one in the kitchen near the door that leads to the garage. Yet there are no signs of motion detectors or any security on the windows."

Gunner shrugged. "Yeah, the house came with this alarm system and it only covers the doors. I never had a reason to look into anything more."

"Well, in light of what you've told me about the attacks, we'll need to better secure the house…just in case."

Gunner yawned and pushed away from the wall. She didn't know why he insisted on showing her around when it was clear that he was exhausted. Since he was a gambler living in Vegas, she imagined he slept all day and hung out in casinos all night. The thought of what he did for a living still irked her. She remembered him being super smart in college. It seemed like such a waste that he hadn't used his knowledge to secure a *real* job. Maxwell had often complained about how hard he had to work for a B, while Gunner breezed through school, carrying a 3.9 grade point average throughout his four years of college. And the way Gunner partied with a stream of women floating in and out of his dorm room, Trinity wondered when he had time to study. What bothered her the most, though, was why he had to become a gambler instead of using his brains for something more productive.

"I trust your judgment regarding the security system," Gunner said, breaking into her thoughts. "Just let me know who to write the check to. Come on and let me show you the rest of the house."

Gunner started out showing Trinity around his home, but when she walked ahead of him, he let her. Following behind her offered a much better view. He didn't know what type of workout routine she did, but whatever she was doing, was definitely working. At five-eight, she was the perfect height for him, with an hourglass figure and long legs that went on for days. Right now, his gaze was on her tight round ass encased in tailored slacks. He couldn't help but imagine how well her butt cheeks would fit into the palms of—

"Okay, so I assume most of the bedrooms are upstairs? I only saw one down here."

"That's correct." He turned suddenly, hoping she hadn't noticed the evidence of how his body had reacted to hers. "I'll go and grab your bags. Your room is upstairs," he called out over his shoulder. He was going to be in a lot of trouble if he got an erection every time she was near him.

Fifteen minutes later, after showing her the three bedrooms with attached bathrooms, he took her to the room that he had prepared for her stay.

"This is lovely." Trinity smiled at him and he wished she would look at him like that more often. "If I didn't know any better, I'd think you had talked to my brother or my mother to find out my favorite colors. The room looks exactly like I would have decorated it."

She ran her hands along the light blue, silk comforter and then onto the footboard of the mahogany sleigh bed. Gunner would never admit to asking Maxwell a few questions regarding her favorite colors and her taste in furniture. Apparently, her brother knew her well. Now, if he could get her to let down her guard some, maybe he could show her the man he had become and not the man she knew back when he was in college.

"Let me show you the last room in the house, and the real reason I purchased this place."

Trinity followed him out of the room and down the hall. He could have given her a room on the other side of the house, but she had given him a speech about being his shadow for the next two months.

"I'm glad you put my room near yours. If I'm going to be guarding you, it's a good idea for me to be as close to you as possible."

Gunner smiled to himself. He was sure she didn't realize how her words sounded to him, but was glad she was okay with the living arrangement.

He pushed open the double doors with as much flair as his exhausted body could muster and ushered her in.

"Welcome to my humble abode."

Trinity laughed when she stepped over the threshold. "There is nothing humble about this space," she said, humor in her voice. This was one of the few rooms that he had hired an interior decorator to create for him. His favorite part, besides the four-poster king-size bed, was the blackout window treatments that were regulated by a remote control. Since he did most of his sleeping during the day, they were necessary and one of the best investments he'd made to date.

"Through the double doors to your left is the main reason I purchased the house."

Gunner's gaze followed the sway of her hips as she glided across the room. He couldn't for the life of him imagine this sexy woman as a cop. Sure, she had no problem saying what was on her mind, and could even be considered aggressive at times, but the thought of her wrestling a criminal to the ground or against a wall to arrest them was mind-boggling. Since she had graduated at the top of her police academy class, he had no doubt that she could handle her business.

"Oh. My. Goodness! This room alone is worth whatever you paid. This is absolutely gorgeous." She gasped and he knew she had spotted the highlight of the luxury space. "Get the heck out of here! It has a sauna, too?"

Gunner stood in the doorway, chuckling at Trinity's expression. Between the four-person sauna, dual vanities, a huge Jacuzzi tub and the enormous size of the bathroom in general, he didn't know which part was his favorite feature. It helped that the space had heated travertine floors and a window near the jetted tub that gave a picturesque view of the mountains. His Realtor had taken him to dozens of homes before finding this one. The lot size of the property was smaller than he wanted, yet he really liked the backyard and pool, but once he saw the master bathroom, he was sold.

"So what do you think of the place?" Gunner asked. He moved away from the door and leaned against the back of the love seat in his bedroom's sitting area.

Trinity stood in the bathroom doorway. "It's nice, but I have to be honest with you. Don't you think it's a little excessive? You're just one person. Why do you need all of this space?"

"You have to understand," he started without looking at her, "I grew up dirt-poor, living in the projects with my parents and my two sisters. We barely had a roof over our heads, let alone three meals a day." He finally glanced up when Trinity moved closer to him. "It's not that I need all of this, but when I was a kid, I had vowed that there were two things that I would have when I made a little cash. A nice, *big* house and the coolest car money could buy."

Trinity laid her hand on his arm and an electric charge shot through him, making him want to pull her to him and never let go.

She quickly snatched her hand away. "Gunner, I'm sorry. I didn't mean to offend you. I have no right to judge you on how you spend your money."

He shrugged. "No harm done. What I have might not be necessary, but it's what I wanted. And sweetheart, I always get what I want."

Chapter 5

Gunner tossed and turned. Despite his fatigue he couldn't sleep, couldn't get comfortable and he knew why. *Trinity.* He'd left her three hours ago to get settled in and familiar with his home. From the moment he spotted her at the airport, his body responded and the tightness in his groin hadn't let up. He would admit that he had been with his share of women, but he could honestly say that none affected him the way she did. There was something about her. He'd felt it years ago and now the web of attraction was stronger than ever.

He jumped when a loud crash came from downstairs. *What the...* He leaped off the bed and hurried into his jeans, not bothering with his briefs or a shirt. His overactive imagination took him on a wild ride of trying to determine what had fallen, hoping Trinity was okay. He rushed out of the room and down the stairs, taking them two at a time.

"Stop!" Trinity stood and dropped the broom.

"What the hell happened?" He froze on the step leading down to the foyer, where Trinity was standing over a pile of broken glass. "Are you all right?"

"Yeah, yeah, I'm fine. I wanted you to stop because when I knocked over your vase, glass flew all over the place. I didn't want you to step on any since you don't have on a shirt." She shook her head. "I mean since you don't have on any shoes," she said, flustered. She quickly turned from him and went back to sweeping up the glass near the large round table in the massive entryway. "I don't understand. You have very little furniture down here, yet you have a table in the middle of the foyer with what *was* an exquisite vase." She bent down and scooped up some of the glass. "And please don't tell me it was a family heirloom or something." She glanced at him, and must have seen the expression on his face. "Oh, no," she groaned. She rocked on her heels and almost tipped back, but caught herself.

"Actually my mother sent it to me. She was doing missionary work in Africa and one of the natives gave it to her for taking such good care of her sick daughter."

"I am so sorry," she groaned again. "I was walking backwards, sizing up the door and the large windows on each side of it. Then I bumped into the table."

"Don't worry about… Ah, damn, Trinity. You're bleeding," he said, seeing blood trickling down her hand. "Stay right there." He darted back up the stairs and slipped into his boots. He jogged down the hall and grabbed the first-aid kit that he kept in the guest bathroom. Hurrying back down the stairs, he ignored the crunching glass beneath his feet and guided Trinity away from the mess and into a smaller bathroom.

"You must've fallen back on some glass." He held her hand under the lukewarm water, trying to determine the source of the blood. He never realized just how small the bathroom was until he had to be in there with another person. And not just any other person—but with Trinity. Being in such close quarters was not a good idea. He fought his overwhelming need to rub his body against hers and determine if she felt as soft as she looked. He almost laughed out loud at the thought. The woman was a security specialist and probably knew several ways to kill a man without even using a weapon. Getting his freak on against her perfectly round butt was a sure way to get pummeled.

"There's a sliver of glass in your hand." He grabbed the tweezers from the first-aid kit and moved her hand closer to the light.

"You do know I can do this my—" Her hand jerked when he dug into her skin to get a grip on the glass. Gunner knew it had to hurt, but she didn't say anything and he kept going. Any other woman would have been crying or squirming around, but not Trinity.

"I think that's it," he finally announced after removing a couple of small pieces, but he double-checked the side of her hand before drying her off.

"Thank you," Trinity said just above a whisper. Gunner had never seen her vulnerable, but the softness in her voice and the shyness he was currently witnessing let him know that there was definitely another side to this independent woman.

As he wrapped her hand, the overwhelming desire to kiss her was getting the best of him. He knew she planned to keep their time together professional, but at this rate, it would be impossible.

He finished with the bandage and then cleaned around the sink. When he followed her out of the tight space, she went back to sweeping up the glass.

"Leave it. I'll take care of it."

"Gunner, that's not necessary. I made this mess. The least I can do is clean it up."

Without saying anything, he took the broom and dustpan away from her. He could tell her hand was bothering her by the way she flinched periodically, but she had yet to complain about pain.

"Are you hungry?" he asked.

A small smile tilted her lips. "Why? It's not like you're going to prepare me a meal. There's not a lick of food in that huge gourmet kitchen of yours."

Gunner laughed and dumped the shards of glass into the trash. "Well, I guess you've probably figured out that the kitchen is just for show."

"And it doesn't look like you eat in there, either. I have never seen a refrigerator so empty."

"I keep saying I'm going to learn to cook, but with so many wonderful restaurants in Vegas…" He shrugged. "I figure, why bother?"

"So why did you need a house with such a massive kitchen?"

Gunner followed her gaze, taking in the ultra-large refrigerator, the Viking rangetop, as well as the double-stacked ovens. "Well, you already know why I purchased the house. The kitchen was a bonus."

She shook her head and he didn't miss the smile forming on her lips. "*If* I were hungry, what did you have in mind?"

"Mexican. I know a great Mexican restaurant where the food is unbelievable. We can either go there or I can have something delivered." He put away the broom and dustpan and rinsed his hands in the kitchen sink.

"Maybe we can eat here," she said. "I want to talk about your home security system and propose some changes."

Gunner studied her for a minute. "Do you need me to take you to the emergency room, have them look at your hand? I can tell it's hurting."

She shook her head. "It'll be okay. Just stinging a little bit, but it's not that serious."

An hour later, they sat at the kitchen table eating everything from chicken enchiladas to Mexican shrimp cocktail. Trinity couldn't believe how much she had eaten and it didn't help that Gunner had a huge appetite and had ordered at least seven different dishes. She had to admit, it was the best Mexican food she'd ever eaten, and that was saying a lot, considering she lived in LA.

"I was surprised to hear that you had left the police force. I remember when you used to say that you were going to be LA's first African-American female chief of police. What happened?"

Trinity moved white rice around on her plate with her fork. "I can't believe you remember that. It seems like a lifetime ago that I said that."

"And it sounded like you were on your way. So what happened?"

Trinity told him how she had been passed over for two different positions. The second time, her supervisor told her that she was too young and too cute to be a lieutenant.

"He'd made comments like that in the past, but this time I couldn't let it go. I really wanted the position and knew it would get me that much closer to the chief's job. I sued the LAPD because I didn't want the same thing to happen to any other women looking to advance her career." Her heart ached as she thought about how she had to leave a job she actually enjoyed. "It was a stressful process, but in the end, I'm glad I went through with it."

"How soon after you won the lawsuit did you open your agency?"

Trinity couldn't remember the last time a man showed true interest in what she did. Most men stayed clear of her, intimidated by her skills as a former SWAT officer. And then there were others who seemed to pick a fight just to see her reaction and to see if she would use some of her defense moves on them.

"I'd been thinking about the agency off and on for years. Celebrities and other wealthy people were often looking to cops who were interested in moonlighting on the side to act as security. After I was approached a couple of times, asking if I'd be interested in providing security for an event or for an individual or group, I knew there was a need." She went to the refrigerator for another bottle of water and grabbed an extra one just in case Gunner wanted another. "So months after I won the lawsuit, I quit my job and opened LEPA."

"That's impressive. I hate that you had to go through all of that crap with the LAPD, but it sounds like going through with the lawsuit might've been a blessing in disguise."

Trinity nodded. It had been, in more ways than one. Not only was she her own boss now, but had it not been for her personal security agency, she might not have ever come in contact with Gunner again. Granted, she still didn't approve of his line of work, but she had to admit that the time she'd spent with him so far was pretty nice.

"Okay, enough about me. Tell me what to expect at the tournament this evening." She set her plate and some of the food containers off to the side. She knew what time they were leaving and that he had a driver that would take them to the casino. Yet outside of that, she didn't have a clue what it was like at a poker tournament.

"Tonight's tournament is at Caesars Palace and will be held in one of their card rooms." He pushed his plate out of the way and crossed his arms on top of the table. Trinity zoned in on his thick forearms, again admiring his perfect physique. How was it that someone who had an appetite as big as his and played poker all day and night could look as though he spent twenty-four hours a day in a gym?

"I assume I'll be able to be in the same room as you. Or are there rules about spectators?"

He shook his head. "Each tournament is set up differently. Tonight, the poker tables will be roped off, but you'll be able to hang out behind the ropes. Now keep in mind there might not be chairs, so that means possibly standing for three to five hours. And I've noticed you're a fan of high heels." He gestured toward her feet.

Trinity glanced at her navy J. Reneé sandals. "You're right, I love heels, and I rarely wear flats. My shoes are usually pretty comfortable, so it shouldn't be a problem."

"This tournament is on a smaller scale than some of those coming up. With this one, you'll get a feel of what to expect over the next couple of months."

Gunner shared the evening's itinerary and Trinity couldn't believe she was going to finally see what all the poker hype was about. Casinos typically weren't among her hangouts, so this evening was going to be interesting, if nothing else.

"There's just one thing that we haven't really talked about in detail."

"And what's that?"

"I don't want anyone to know that you're my bodyguard."

"That shouldn't be a problem. I'll stay close without being too obvious and I'll be dressed like everyone else. They'll just think I'm one of your friends."

"Yeah, about that." His intense dark eyes met hers. "Going forward, I want people we come in contact with to think that you're more than a friend. If anyone asks, tell them that you're my woman."

Chapter 6

Trinity sat at a small table with two other onlookers near where Gunner was playing. Less than six feet away from him, she had an excellent view of his table. She wasn't sure whom he had talked to in order to get her a prime spot and a table, but it was clear that he had a lot of pull in the circuit.

Tell them that you're my woman. Gunner's words came back to her. She at first balked at the idea, thinking there was no way she'd pretend to be his girlfriend. Once he explained that he would prefer people to not know that he had a bodyguard, she gave in to the request. She could understand how a macho guy like Gunner felt, needing to hire someone to watch his back.

From the moment the driver picked them up from the house, Gunner had fallen into the role of doting boyfriend. Part of her felt like the girl who got to date the captain of the football team. He'd been so attentive, making her feel special, a little giddy even. But the other part of her, the businesswoman part of her, reminded herself that this was an assignment and Gunner was her client. It would be really easy to fall for his good looks and his charm. Yet she had no intention of being among the long line of broken hearts that Gunner left behind. She'd pretend to be his girlfriend, but as far as she was concerned, she was only his bodyguard.

Trinity glanced back at Gunner's table. Slouched in his seat, which seemed to be his standard way of sitting, wearing that same ratty baseball cap pulled low over his eyes, it was clear that he took the game seriously. This whole setup with him seemed so surreal. Never in a million years would she have imagined herself being this up close and personal with Gunner Brooks, and hired to protect him.

Another person at the table where Gunner played stood to leave. Light bounced off the gold, shiny object that looked like a key chain he'd been twirling between his fingers throughout the game. Trinity assumed it was some type of good-luck charm. She didn't miss how each of the players seemed to have some type of ritual or idiosyncrasy about themselves that stood out. For Gunner, it was the way he wore his cap low over his eyes. Except for when he placed a bet, his moves were barely perceptible and it amazed her how he could sit so still for long periods of time.

Gunner's chip stack continued to grow. There were only three other people besides him remaining at his table. Trinity couldn't help but smile. He seemed so unassuming, so unlike she had imagined. When she researched him, it became clear that he was well respected amongst other players. She hadn't found any skeletons—no bad press, no girlfriend drama, not even a speeding ticket. With his squeaky-clean dossier, Gunner could be the poster boy for professional gambling. She was still anti-gambling, but was actually enjoying watching him play. Yet she wouldn't admit it to him or anyone else. It seemed this assignment would be easier than she expected.

A half an hour later, a commotion at the entrance closest to Trinity caught her attention. She wasn't sure what was going on, but when she saw several security people run past the door, she decided to check things out. One quick glance at Gunner showed her he was focused on the cards and she decided that he would be fine for a few minutes.

By the time she made it into the hallway, a small crowd of people had gathered at the end of the hall near the restrooms. It appeared that whatever had happened was over, but she still moved in closer to see what the upheaval was about.

"When I walked in, he was sprawled out on the floor, blood seeping from a gash on the back of his head," a man told a police officer, who was quickly taking notes. "There was no one else in the bathroom."

At that moment, the victim was wheeled out of the restroom by the EMTs, a bandage wrapped bandana-style around his head. Whatever had happened, Trinity was glad to see that the man was alive—banged up, but alive.

"Hey, that's Jeff Conrad!" a bystander yelled out. "Aw, man, he doesn't look too good. He's probably going to miss the next round."

"That's messed up," the man standing near him said.

"They were talking about him walking away with the PPO championship this year."

Trinity stood near the scene for a few minutes longer. Glancing around, she wasn't looking for anything in particular, but she noticed there were a number of cameras in the area. They would have picked up something. The crowd slowly thinned out and she moved closer to the restrooms. She had hoped to get a better idea of what happened to that Conrad guy, but based on the little that she'd overheard from the cops, they didn't really have anything. Gunner's concerns might have merit, but she'd be damned if anything happened to him on her watch.

Trinity turned to leave the area when she noticed something green and sparkly near the men's bathroom door. She picked it up and moved it around in the center of her palm. The size of a thumbtack, the expensive-looking stone, possibly a real emerald, seemed familiar. *I've seen this before*, she thought. Her memory was pretty good, but for the life of her she couldn't determine whether she'd seen it on someone or on an object.

She shrugged and dropped the stone into the side pocket of her handbag. "I'm sure it'll come to me."

Gunner glanced around, wondering where Trinity had disappeared to. Though his chip count was increasing and he was in the lead at his table, his concentration wasn't what it should be. He could blame it on exhaustion from participating in several tournaments in the last couple of days, but he knew better. It was Trinity. Never had he invited a woman to a tournament and now he remembered why—too distracting. He had glanced at her a few times; mostly, she was looking around the room. He wondered what she thought. It had been clear when he met with her in LA that she wasn't a fan of gambling, or maybe she wasn't a fan of him. He still wasn't sure.

Just as he was about to place his bet, he saw her re-enter the card room. Without moving his head, so as not to bring attention to himself, his gaze followed her smooth glide across the room. Wearing a black blouse with a plunging neckline and black skintight pants wrapped around her voluptuous curves, she drew the attention of every man she passed, and Gunner could barely contain his annoyance. He was definitely going to have to talk to her about her sexy attire.

She finally made it back to her seat. Part of him wanted to strap her down in it, while the other part of him wanted her on his lap to help hide the proof of his desire for her.

Gunner took a few cleansing breaths, trying to rid his head of the erotic thoughts going through his mind. But then his gaze met hers and the slowly burning flame that was simmering in his gut turned into a roaring fire when she smiled at him.

Damn.

"You gon' play poker, Brooks, or are you going to keep gaping at the hottie with the perky assets over there?" Roman Jeers asked. Gunner wanted to leap over the table and wipe the smug look off his nemesis's face. A trash talker to the ninth degree, Roman always had something to say. But in this case, he was right. Gunner needed to keep his head in the game and not on Trinity's *assets*; otherwise, he could be one of the next ones to leave the table empty-handed.

He lifted the corner of his cards, careful to keep

them covered, and glanced at his hand. *Four of a kind.* He wanted this game to be over, and the way it looked, at least one person would be leaving after this round. The player sitting directly across from him was clearly on the brink of losing. If his short stack of chips wasn't a clue, then the beads of sweat on his forehead, shining like a neon sign blinking *busted*, were a sure giveaway. Gunner placed his bet, raising the stakes, and waited.

Hours later, Gunner walked into the house and tossed his keys on the counter. He'd made out well at the table, but finding out about Jeff's attack had ruined the evening. *This shit is getting too close to home.* In all the years of playing poker, never had there been a time when he'd had to look over his shoulder for fear of someone doing him harm. He now had no doubt that someone was picking off poker players—one by one.

"Thanks, Max," Gunner heard Trinity say into her cell phone. "Definitely keep me posted on anything you find out."

"So does it look like the cops are going to take this situation a little more seriously?"

Trinity sighed and sat on one of the bar stools. "Right now, they don't have much to go on. There were no witnesses. Max is going to see if they can get ahold of the videos near the restroom, and hopefully they'll reveal something. There's not much more—"

"He's the third player to be attacked in the last few weeks and it looks like he's out for the season. Are the cops waiting until someone is killed before they take this mess seriously?" He didn't want to hear anything about them not being able to do something because of no leads or lack of evidence. He just wanted to play poker without worrying if he was next on someone's list.

Gunner rolled his shoulders, took a deep breath, and then released it. Right now, he needed to take his mind off of poker, the incidents and more important, the beautiful woman standing before him—Trinity. He wanted to explore the attraction between them, but if he made a move on her now, he would ruin any chance of there ever being more between them.

He had to get rid of some of his pent-up stress, and there were only a couple of ways to do that. One of those was sex, but he knew that wasn't going to happen, at least not with the woman he wanted. So he did what he'd done for the past few months. He grabbed a bottle of water from the refrigerator and headed for his home gym.

He moved across the room, but Trinity stopped him when she placed a hand on his arm.

He stood motionless, staring down at her small hand, trying not to show how her touch affected him. His concentration had been shot to hell for most of the evening, thanks to her presence. Now, her touch sent a scorching heat through his body and it took everything within him not to pull her into his arms and taste her inviting lips.

Apparently, she felt the same spark of desire. She quickly withdrew her hand.

"Don't worry. I'm not going to let anything happen to you," she said.

The thought of a woman telling him that she was going to protect him didn't sit right with Gunner. Sure, he had wanted a female bodyguard, but that part of his idea had stemmed from wanting Trinity and him to get reacquainted.

"Thanks," he mumbled and walked away.

"Before you go." He stopped again and faced her. "I'd like to teach you a few self-defense moves, just in case you ever find yourself in a tough situation and need to protect yourself."

A bark of laughter erupted from him. "*You're* going to show *me* some moves?" When she put her hands on her hips and shifted her weight to one leg, scowling, he stopped laughing. His mouth dropped open. "You're serious?"

"I'm dead serious." She removed the lightweight jacket and revealed the sexy black blouse that had almost cost him a loss tonight. Tossing her jacket to one of the kitchen chairs, she moved into the family room and kicked off her killer high heels. "Gunner, this is part of my job. This is what I do." She glanced back at him, still standing in the kitchen, dumbfounded.

He analyzed her for a moment. The way his body ached for her, it would be best for him to head to his home gym as originally planned. But there was a stronger force pushing him toward her and he was powerless to resist.

"So what do you say? Are you going to let me teach you some moves?"

He set his bottle of water on the kitchen counter and went to her. "Sweetheart, I have moves that you haven't seen or experienced before."

Before she could respond, his mouth covered hers with a hunger that had built up since the first day she had stepped into his dorm room all those years ago. It had taken everything within him not to seize what he wanted back then, but now he couldn't help himself. He kissed her deeply and thoroughly, drinking in the sweetness of her lips, succumbing to the power she had over him.

His hands scaled down the sides of her hips and pulled her curvy body close. He had no doubt that she felt the length of his desire pressing against her pelvis. The lower part of his body moved of its own accord as he ground against her. His heart pounded so loudly within his chest, he was sure she could hear it. None of his fantasies of having her in his arms matched the reality of this moment. He heard himself moan and then her body went rigid, as if she was suddenly coming to her senses.

"Oh, my God," she whispered and pushed him away. "What are you doing?" she said, her hand hovering near her mouth, her eyes wild and accusing.

"If you don't know, apparently I wasn't doing it right."

"Don't get cute! You know what I'm talking about." She ran her hands through her shoulder-length hair and paced around the room. She stopped and glared at him. "I don't know what possessed you to kiss me, but you had better make sure it doesn't happen again."

"I'm attracted to you and, based on that kiss, I'd say the feelings are mutual. So I did what I've longed to do for years. And I must say, it was even more amazing than I imagined it would be."

"Like I said, it can't happen again," she huffed. "Otherwise, I'm going to have to put someone else on this assignment."

Now she had his attention. With two long strides,

he stood before her and gently grabbed her chin, forcing her to meet his gaze.

"We have an agreement." He leaned in close, but stopped just before his lips touched hers. "And if I wanted someone else to guard me, I would have hired someone else. I want *you*. Besides, sweetheart, we signed a contract. You're mine for two months."

Days later, Trinity still felt the effects of Gunner's kiss. She subconsciously touched her lips. He'd been correct. Their attraction was mutual, but she had no intention of acting on it. She was there to do a job and that was what she intended to do.

Trinity grabbed her cell phone from the table near the bed and plopped down in the overstuffed chair near the window in her bedroom. It was quickly becoming her favorite spot in the house. Whenever Gunner was hanging out in his game room or catching up on sleep, she hung out in her room. She didn't want to spend any more time in his presence than she had to.

She dialed her mother's number.

"Hello."

"Hey, Mom, what are you up to?"

"Hi, baby, I'm glad to hear from you," Trinity's mother said in greeting, pots banging in the background. "I'm fine. Were your ears burning? I was just talking about you."

She curled her legs underneath her and rested her head against the back of the comfortable chair.

"Okay, Mom, who were you talking to and what were you saying about me?" Lately her mother insisted on conspiring with some of her girlfriends who had sons. She was determined to get Trinity married, claiming it was time her daughter gave her some grand-babies.

"Actually, Gwen was telling me that her oldest son has moved back to LA for a job with the government. She's throwing a dinner party for him once he gets settled and she invited you and me."

"I can't remember the last time I saw Auntie Gwen, so I'm surprised that she invited me." Trinity toyed with a loose thread on the chair. It was a shame her love life was so pitiful that her mother had to play matchmaker. "Are you sure this is not one of your and Auntie Gwen's attempts at matchmaking? Because you know how I feel about that. I can find my own man."

"Well, why haven't you? It's not like you're getting any younger. I'd like to have some grandchildren before you and your brother put me into the ground."

Though Trinity knew that everyone had to die at some point, she hated when her mother talked about dying. "I'm only twenty-eight. There's plenty of time to get married and still have children."

"Humph, if you say so." Trinity heard more pots clattering around and then water running. Despite the fact that she and Maxwell no longer lived at home, her mother still prepared a large Sunday dinner. She always invited some of her friends over to eat with her. "So, how is Vegas and that handsome Gunner Brooks?"

"It's okay and he's fine." Actually, he was more than *fine*, but no way would Trinity tell her mother that. "My only complaint is the heat."

"Are we talking weather heat, or the heat between you and Gunner?"

Trinity's mouth dropped open. "Mom!"

"Don't 'Mom' me. When you two were younger, I saw the way you looked at each other."

Trinity placed her feet on the floor and leaned forward, her elbows on her thighs. "I think you've been reading too many of those romance novels you have stashed near your bed. There is nothing between Gunner and me. Never has been, never will be."

Trinity ignored the little voice in the back of her head that chanted, *Liar, liar, liar.* Sure, she knew something was going on between her and Gunner, but she wasn't ready to accept the strong feelings between them.

"I know what I saw, baby. I never said anything because I figured if it was meant to be, it would be. And I'm starting to think it's meant to be."

"Mom."

"You could do a lot worse. He's good-looking, wealthy and a real sweetheart. Any mother would love to have him as a son-in-law."

Trinity rolled her eyes. "Mom, you know I can't stand gamblers. You of all people should understand that."

Silence filled the phone line and Trinity wondered if she'd gone too far. They rarely talked about her father and his gambling problem.

"I haven't seen Gunner in months. You make sure you tell him that I said the next time he's in LA, I want to see him."

"Mom, I'm sorry if I said too much, but I don't want to go through what you went through with Dad. I don't want my children to experience disappointment after disappointment because my husband gambled away everything we own. You might have been able to put up with that type of lifestyle, but I can't. I will never—"

"That's enough, Trinity Marie Layton! I will not have you bad-mouthing your father. God rest his soul. You only remember a small part of who your father was. Apparently you don't remember the number of times he stayed home from work to care for you when you were sick. You probably don't remember how he used to take our next-door neighbor to the hospital every day. For two weeks straight he would come home from his third-shift job and take Lillian to see her husband who was in a coma."

Trinity felt like scum when she heard her mother quietly crying. She never could understand her mother's rationale for staying in the marriage as long as she had. Clearly, there was a side of her father that Trinity never had a chance to know.

"I loved your father with all of my heart. No, he wasn't perfect, but neither was I. He had aspirations of being a professional poker player like Gunner, but things didn't work out for your father the way they have for Gunner." Her mother sniffed. "At first he made enough money gambling for us to live off of. He paid cash for the house we were living in and had even bought the car that I drove around in."

This revelation shocked Trinity. She had no idea her father had ever been successful gambling. Yet it still didn't change her mind about him. He should have stopped while he was ahead, but no, he gambled away everything.

"It took a while for your father and me to realize that his gambling had spiraled out of control and that he was losing more than he was winning. And just so that you know, I never would have left your father had he not insisted."

"What?" Trinity thought her mother had finally left the marriage because she couldn't take the gambling and drinking any longer.

"When I married your father, I married him for better or for worse. I married the man who I fell madly in love with and I had every intention of honoring my vows. Besides the gambling and drinking, your father was the sweetest, most compassionate and loving man I have ever known. He insisted I leave Vegas, taking you and your brother with me, because he was dying."

Trinity fell back against her chair. Another fact about her father she hadn't known. How could her parents keep something like this from her? She wondered if Max knew. Had he kept this from her, as well?

"When you were six, he was diagnosed with mesothelioma. He didn't want us around to watch him die. It was hearing the news about the disease that caused him to start drinking, not the gambling."

Again, Trinity was stunned. Her head swam with all of this new information. Suddenly she didn't know what to think about her father. But the things she did know and remember still were at the forefront of her mind.

"You father lived much longer than he or the doctors had expected, but he could never get his life back on track. I fault myself because I…we should have stayed. We left him at a time when he needed family the most and he died alone. I don't know if I'll ever be able to fully forgive myself."

Trinity stood and paced around the room. "You can't blame yourself." All that her mother had shared shocked her, but it wasn't her mother's fault. "Mom, please don't blame yourself for what happened to Daddy. You were a great wife and you're the best mom a girl could have." Trinity fanned her eyes, trying hard not to cry. She wasn't the most compassionate person in the world, but it was as if her mother's emotional pain transferred through the telephone and gripped Trinity like a vice.

"Baby, I am so sorry for dumping all of that on you. I just don't want you to discount a man like Gunner because of who you think your father was. If the attraction I saw between you and Gunner years ago is still there, you owe it to yourself to see where it might take you."

"Mom…"

"Hear me out, Trinity. I know you think I'm too old and out of touch to know how it feels to be attracted to someone, but I'm not. I suggest you get to know who Gunner the man is and don't judge him solely on what he does for a living."

Trinity and her mother talked for a few minutes longer until her mother told her that she had to get off the telephone because she had an afternoon date with a guy she met at bingo.

Trinity stood at the window in her room, replaying the conversation with her mother. Granted, she was glad to know that her father wasn't the lowlife that she'd once thought. Yet the fact they'd been homeless for a period weighed heavily on her mind. That she couldn't forget.

Trinity turned from the window and glanced at her watch. It was two in the afternoon and she knew that

Gunner had a tournament at five. What she didn't know was when he needed to leave home to get there on time.

Trinity went downstairs, still in awe of the size of his home. She couldn't imagine living in such a large place alone. She understood why he'd purchased the mini-mansion, but it still seemed like such a waste.

She knocked on the closed door of his game room.

"Come in."

Trinity stepped in and found Gunner watching a flat-screen television mounted on the wall over the slot machines. He sat at one of the four gaming tables in the room; a poker game on the screen held his attention. During the tour of his home that he'd given her the first day she arrived, he had told her that his game room was one of his favorite rooms in the house. It looked like a mini casino. Slot machines lined the perimeter of the room and various gaming tables occupied every available floor space in the center.

She moved farther into the room. "Most people have home offices or maybe even a craft room in their house, but you've given a whole new meaning to 'game room.' I have to ask, is all of this really necessary? I could see having a poker table, but this is a bit much." She stretched out her arms, emphasizing all of his toys in the room. "Slot machines, gaming tables...it seems like such a waste of money."

Gunner said nothing. His attention was no longer on the television screen. Instead, he toyed with a few chips on the table he was sitting at. As he twirled the chips between his long, tapered fingers, Trinity stood mesmerized at the rhythm he created with the simple movement. She couldn't tell if he was thinking or ignoring her.

"I just don't understand how you people can spend so much time doing something as meaningless as gambling."

He stopped, set the chips on the table, and finally looked at her. Seconds ticked by before he spoke. "So you think what I do for a living is meaningless?" he asked quietly.

Trinity didn't miss the venomous edge in his tone. He stood slowly, his steely gaze never leaving her face. The air pressure in the room shifted. The pounding in her chest increased in speed as he moved toward her. She swallowed hard, afraid that her big mouth had once again said too much.

Chapter 7

The first prickles of his anger rose to the surface. Gunner wasn't quite sure where her distaste for what he did for a living originated, but he'd be damned if he'd let her put down something she clearly had no clue about.

"I'm not sure what you mean by *you people*, but I am a *professional* poker player. I might gamble for a living, but I have worked my ass off to be the best at what I do. This might seem a little excessive to you, but this is a part of my job. I have recreated an environment that I am most comfortable in, an environment that has helped me to make more money than most people can even dream of. And the best part— I'm doing what I love to do."

"Gunner, I—"

"So don't come in here lumping what I do on a professional level with some of those two-bit gamblers out here." He eased toward her, his voice low and taut with anger. "Don't confuse me with those who use their family's life savings or the grocery money, hoping to triple those few dollars by hanging out in the casinos." When he got in her face, his voice went deeper, rage still lacing each word. "And most important, you don't even know me. How are you going to come into my home and judge how I make a living—a damn good living at that?"

Gunner abruptly turned away, trying to slow his rapid heartbeat. Rarely did he let the prejudices of others regarding his career get to him, but he'd had enough. He could blame his outburst on exhaustion, but he knew it was more than that. From the day he'd first met with Trinity at her office in LA, he'd sensed some underlying animosity toward him. He assumed it was because she thought he was still the same old selfish bastard he had been back in college, chasing anything in a skirt. But for the past week, her periodic snide remarks regarding gambling proved that she had a problem with the sport, not just him.

He clenched his jaw to keep from saying anything else to her. He didn't anger often, and he sure as hell didn't raise his voice at women, but he didn't like her attitude regarding his career.

"Gunner. I'm—"

He lifted his hand and strolled to the door. "Save it, Trinity. The car will be here in an hour. Be ready."

Gunner walked into his bedroom and slammed the door. Fury he hadn't felt in years hammered in his gut and he wanted to hit something, anything. He snatched the lamp from his bedside table and hurled it across the room, not caring about the ear-piercing sound that came when it hit the wall or the shards of glass littering the carpet.

Who the hell does she think she is?

He charged into the bathroom. The door crashed into the wall and he wasted no time in stripping off his clothes. Tossing the lamp had done nothing to alleviate the rage that gripped him. From the day he went pro, he'd had to deal with the same crap Trinity was spewing moments ago, but this time…this time it was different. Her words cut deep. They were like salt in an open wound, stinging something fierce and aggravating the hell out of him.

He turned the shower on full blast. The colder the water was, the better it would be in taming the madness storming through his veins. He had one hour to calm the hell down and get his head ready for tonight.

Trinity grabbed hold of one of the chairs, her hands gripping the back of the seat. Gunner had been nothing but nice to her since the moment he'd picked her up from the airport, and what did she do? Insult him… in his home.

What is wrong with me?

She startled when she heard his door slam and jumped when a loud crash came soon after. To say he was mad would be an understatement. She played the words that she'd said to him over and over in her mind, trying to figure out which remark had set him off. She shook her head, disgusted at her holier-than-thou attitude. She was way out of line. Her opinion of poker players or gambling didn't matter. He'd hired her to do a job, not give a commentary on what she thought of how he spent money or the way he chose to live his life.

Stupid, stupid, stupid, she chanted as she headed out of the game room and up the stairs. *I have to make this right.*

She stopped in front of his bedroom door, her hand fisted and ready to knock. But what would she say? What could she say? *I'm a jerk. Please forgive me. I didn't mean anything by what I said to you?* She lowered her hand. She couldn't say any of that. Though it was none of her business what he did with his money or that he was a gambler, she still felt that what he had was excessive. Sure, it was his money, and maybe he did work hard for it and could do whatever the heck he wanted, but her opinion was her opinion. If she apologized for anything, it would be for overstepping her place. He was a grown man. Technically, she was his employee and had no business commenting on anything. It was just that they had gotten a little friendly and she had temporarily forgotten herself. It wouldn't happen again.

She turned from his door and walked across the hall to the bedroom she was using, deciding she would apologize when she saw him.

They walked into the house hours later and Gunner tossed his keys onto the breakfast bar. Walking through the first floor of the house, he turned on the lights. His mind was still on how lousily he had played. As a matter of fact, he couldn't remember the last time he'd played as poorly as he had tonight.

"Are you going to give me the silent treatment for the rest of this assignment?" Trinity asked from behind him as he headed for the stairs.

Gunner stopped and faced her. "No. I didn't realize I was giving you the silent treatment," he lied.

Trinity gave him a *yeah, right* look, her hands sliding to her hips. "I have apologized and I'm sorry if our disagreement affected your game tonight. I had no idea—"

Gunner eased toward her. "Disagreement? Is that what you call it?" he asked, but didn't give her a chance to finish. "You insult me in my home, judge me based on…hell, I don't even know, and the crazy thing is, it doesn't seem like you see anything wrong with any of it."

At least she had the decency to look contrite when she dropped her arms to her sides. He knew Trinity was a decent person, but he had no idea what her beef was about gambling. And because he was tired, frustrated and horny as hell, right now he didn't really care. He planned to take another cold shower, and then go to bed.

"I don't know what else to say."

Their eyes met. Despite his disappointment in her, the attraction he felt for her was stronger than ever, making him pissed at himself. How could someone so beautiful and normally kind be so judgmental? And how could he be jonesing for her when he knew she didn't respect him or his choice of career? Part of him wanted to send her home and watch his own back. There was another part of him that wanted to understand the attitude behind her animosity toward gamblers and get to know her better.

He took off his baseball cap and rubbed his head. It was two o'clock in the morning, too late for any type of conversation as far as he was concerned.

"You don't have to say anything else. Let's just forget it. We have to coexist for the next couple of months. We can agree to disagree about what I do for a living and how I spend my money."

Her shoulders dropped. "Gunner, I was out of line. I feel awful about what I said and I hope you can forgive me if it was because of me that you lost tonight."

"Trinity, what do you want me to say?"

"I want you to say that you forgive me."

"Fine. I forgive you. Now can we go to bed… separately?" he added when she lifted an eyebrow in question.

"I'd like motion detectors throughout the house on both levels," Trinity explained days later as she escorted the installation technician back to the first floor of Gunner's home. The company had great reviews and came recommended by a friend of hers, but there was something about the guy that creeped her out.

"If you decide to go with our company, we should be able to start the day after tomorrow."

"Sean, what would it take to start and complete the project today?" Gunner had told her to get what she thought was best and that money wasn't an issue.

For the past couple of days, they had done as he suggested—coexisted. But she had to admit that she missed the lighter, carefree side of him. For the most part, he'd been keeping things professional. Part of her was happy about that, but the other part of her missed the sexual innuendos and the heated looks he used to give her.

Trinity returned her attention to her visitor. Sean rubbed his chin and eyed her with a slight smile on his lips, his gaze raking boldly down her body, desire brimming in his beady little eyes. "Oh, I don't know," he said slowly. "You're asking for a lot and I can tell you now, it's not going to be cheap." He licked his lips, his gaze lingering on her breasts.

"How much?" *You horny jerk.* She couldn't stand men who thought they were all that, and this guy clearly wasn't. Average height, thinning hair and a slight beer belly—there was nothing about him that interested her. He was definitely not her type, although lately she wasn't sure what that was.

"Well, maybe we can go to breakfast and I can break down the cost. I'm sure we can come to an amicable agreement." He stepped closer and Trinity almost burst out laughing. Was he serious? Did he honestly think she wanted him?

Gunner chose that moment to come down the stairs, pulling his T-shirt over his head, but not before Trinity had a chance to witness flat abs covered in smooth dark chocolate. He was wearing his usual uniform: T-shirt with well-worn jeans and yet another pair of Timberlands, navy blue ones. Ruggedly handsome, the man could probably make raggedy overalls look good. *Well, I guess I know what my type is.*

"Morning," Gunner said, glancing at Sean before turning his full attention to Trinity. She met his gaze and her pulse picked up speed. Normally his dark eyes were shielded by his baseball cap, but not this morning. His low haircut looked as if he'd been running his fingers through it and his mustache and goatee were perfectly trimmed. "So what's going on?"

"Hey, how you doing? I'm Sean with King's Security." He shook Gunner's hand and then whipped out his business card. "My company will be install-ing your—"

"Actually, I think we're going to go with someone else," Trinity cut in. She made her way to the door and opened it.

"Now, wait a minute," Sean said. "A moment ago you were asking me when we could start."

"Yeah, that was before you tried to proposition me."

"What?" Gunner chimed in, the one word ricochet-ing off the walls of the semi-empty room.

Sean shot his hands out in defense when Gunner looked as if he was going to throttle him. Surprised by his response and the way he glared at the security guy, Trinity prepared herself just in case she had to step in.

"Wait, it wasn't like that." Sean turned panicked eyes to Trinity when Gunner moved in closer. "I defi-nitely didn't mean for anything I might have said to sound like an indecent proposition. I only—"

"You know what?" Trinity said. "You should prob-ably go."

When he didn't move through the opened door, Gunner stepped to him.

"Man, get the hell out of my house."

The moment Trinity closed the door behind Sean, Gunner said, "I don't think it's a good idea for you to meet with these people by yourself."

Trinity released a humorless laugh and followed him into the kitchen. "I see you have jokes this morning. Because if you're implying that it's not *safe* for me to meet with them alone, I think you should be more wor-ried about them than me. I'm a *trained* security spe-cialist. I can take care of myself."

Gunner pulled a carton of orange juice from the

refrigerator and set it on the counter before grabbing a glass. "That might be, but I don't feel comfortable knowing that you'll be subjected to others who might try to proposition you."

Trinity waved him off. "I'm sure that was an isolated incident. I'm meeting with two more security companies this morning, and one of them comes highly recommended."

Gunner eyed her over the rim of his glass. His gaze slid slowly down her body. First, she had to endure that pervert Sean's perusal of her body, now Gunner's. *What the heck is wrong with these men today?*

She looked down at her attire. "What? Why are you looking at me like that?"

He shrugged. "Just wondering why you're dressed like that."

Her eyebrows drew together. "Like what?" As far as she was concerned, she looked fine in a white off-the-shoulder blouse and her favorite black trouser jeans with comfortable two-inch red heels. "What's wrong with my outfit?"

He set his glass on the table and approached her with that lazy gait that she found sexy as hell. Everything about the man oozed sex appeal. He looped his finger through one of her belt loops and pulled her toward him. His touch, even though it was not against her skin, sent a wicked sensation through her body and heat to her most private body parts. *Good Lord*. It was no wonder women had been so attracted to him back in college. The man was downright irresistible.

Trinity held her breath, afraid that he would kiss her. Actually, that wasn't what worried her. What really bothered her was that if his lips touched hers, she

Sharon C. Cooper 87

wouldn't be able to resist kissing him back. Maybe he really had forgiven her for her outburst the other day. She hoped so, but she also hoped he wasn't getting the wrong idea about them.

"Sweetheart, you look as if you're about to go clubbing with some of your girlfriends." The desire in his eyes as he looked her over once more had a way different effect on her than when Sean had let his degenerate gaze travel down her body. "This little number you're wearing is way too sexy for meeting with what will probably be men."

Trinity gently pushed against his hard pecs and freed herself from his loose grip. Besides, his nearness was making her hot as hell, despite the fact that the air conditioner was on full blast.

"Thanks for the tip, but our agreement didn't include you telling me what to wear and what not to wear. This is how I always dress and I'm comfortable."

"Even so, what time are the next two appointments? I might want to hear what they have to say about my home's security system."

Just then, the doorbell rang.

Gunner didn't know how he was going to get through the next couple of months with this sexy vixen living under his roof. The last two days had been tolerable, especially since they didn't talk about their *disagreement* from the other day and he had to admit that he was enjoying her company. But having her stay with him 24/7 seemed like a good idea at first, but now, as he watched her luscious derriere, wrapped in too-tight jeans, practically glide to the door, he wasn't so sure. At this rate, he was going to be in a constant state of arousal for the next couple of months.

"Gunner," Trinity called out as she approached the kitchen. Gunner looked up just as she entered. "This is Roberto. His organization is the sister company to one I use in LA," she said of the man who stepped from behind her. Gunner didn't miss the way the guy eyed Trinity's ass. If this was the type of attention she attracted, Gunner knew he was in for a few fights, either with her or her admirers, before this arrangement was over. Trinity might not have been his woman for real, but damn if he wasn't jealous of the attention she received. Even now, he wanted to poke the guy's eyes out and then lock Trinity up in a room somewhere.

Gunner greeted the guy, making sure to put a little something extra in his handshake. When Roberto's gaze met Gunner's, there was definitely an understanding between them. He didn't want this guy to have any ideas about getting with Trinity. Gunner and Trinity still needed to work through some things, but after spending the past couple of days together without incident, he was encouraged that they could get past whatever issue Trinity had with him.

"Okay, Roberto," Trinity laid a hand on the man's arm, but narrowed her eyes at Gunner. "Let me show you around."

Gunner followed them from room to room, not caring that Trinity was giving him the evil eye. Whether she could handle herself or not, he wasn't leaving her alone with any of these guys.

A couple of hours later, after the last of Trinity's appointments had come and gone, Trinity let him have it.

"You are unbelievable!" She stormed into the

kitchen where he was unloading lunch that he'd had delivered from a nearby deli. "I can't believe the way you were acting. What is wrong with you?"

"Besides being hungry, nothing's wrong with me." He grabbed a couple of plates and utensils. He placed them on top of the glass dinette table that was in the corner of the kitchen. "Are you ready to eat?" he asked.

She stood next to the table, her hands on her hips and her blouse stretched across her ample breasts. If she knew how much her pose was turning him on, she'd fold her arms across her chest and hide her luscious mounds. Apparently, she had no idea just how sexy she was.

"This whole little wrapping your arms around my waist, calling me sweetheart and all the other crap was very unnecessary." He pulled out the kitchen chair for her to sit down and she rolled her eyes at him, but sat anyway. "I don't know why you felt a need to playact that something was going on between us. I agreed to pretend to be your woman when we're out and about, but we're at home. Those guys were just trying to make a sell. They were not interested in me. So your behavior was unwarranted."

"I disagree." He took a bite of his grilled chicken sandwich. "You might not have noticed, but those guys were definitely checking you out."

"And what's it to you?" She picked at her salad, not making eye contact. "You and I have a business agreement and *nothing* else."

There was definitely something else, but Gunner didn't bother voicing that fact. At some point, she was going to let her guard down and give in to the sexual charge that was between them.

She finally looked up, but only for a second. After the kiss they shared the other day, he knew without a doubt that they were attracted to each other. She could try to fight if she wanted to, but he always went after what he wanted. He had no intention of fighting the inevitable. They would be together.

Chapter 8

"So how's it going with having Trinity here?" Maxwell asked Gunner as they lounged in the theater room, watching an NBA game on the 120-inch screen.

"It's okay." Gunner shoved a handful of popcorn into his mouth before continuing. "We had some heated words a few days after she arrived, but lately we've been getting along fine."

"What do you mean by 'heated words'?"

Gunner was a private person for the most part. He and Maxwell were good friends, but it felt a little weird discussing Trinity with her brother. Then again, maybe Max could shed some light on what Trinity had against gamblers.

"Your sister seems to have a problem with my career choice and how I spend my money."

Maxwell frowned and shook his head. "That girl," he said under his breath.

"I take it your silence means you know something about the subject."

"Her issues stem from our past, our childhood. I think it would be better if you talked to her about this."

When Maxwell left, Gunner asked Trinity if they could talk. He was definitely interested in her, but he was more curious than ever to find out what she had against him and gambling.

"Hey, everything okay?" she asked when she walked into the kitchen wearing a yellow fitted tank top and white shorts that stopped midthigh, showing off her amazing, long legs.

Even after a couple of weeks together, Gunner still couldn't get used to how *hot* she was.

He pulled out one of the kitchen chairs. "Have a seat." He took the seat across from her and folded his hands on top of the table in front of him.

"Why do you hate me and gambling so much?" He was never one for tiptoeing around a situation.

She stared at him for a minute, but then placed her elbows on top of the table and rubbed her forehead. When she didn't speak, he reached out and touched her arm.

"Talk to me."

Trinity sighed loudly before she spoke. "I owe you an apology. A for-real apology." Her voice was so quiet, Gunner almost missed what she'd said. "I had no right to judge you. It's just that…"

She stood abruptly and walked over to the breakfast bar, her attention on Gunner.

She continued to stare at him, tears pooled in her eyes as she twisted her hands together in front of her. He had no idea what she'd planned to share, but whatever it was had to be troubling. She was usually so confident and full of life that expressing her feelings never seemed to be a problem for her, until now.

"It's just what?" He slowly approached her. "What is it? Why are you so against me and what I do?" He lifted his hand to touch her, but lowered it, afraid she would pull away. Whatever was bothering her, they needed to hash it out now. There was no way he was going through the next couple of months with this tension between them.

She stepped away from him, rubbing her bare arms, and moving around the center island until she stood on the other side of the room. Trinity stopped and leaned against the counter.

"My father was a gambler...and as far as I'm concerned, the gambling led to homelessness, a drinking problem...and ultimately his death."

Damn. Gunner knew a little about her and Maxwell's upbringing, but apparently, Maxwell had left out a few things. All Gunner knew is that they had lived in Vegas until Maxwell was around eight or nine, then their mother moved them to LA when she'd left their father.

"When I was a little girl, I thought my father could do no wrong. He was big, strong, and made me feel as if I were the luckiest girl in the world." She stood at the patio doors, looking out into the backyard. "When I turned five, my mother threw me a birthday party. She claims I had a party every year, but this is the only one that I remember as clear as if it were yesterday. All of my friends were there and for weeks I had bragged about how wonderful the party would be and that my daddy was buying me a brand-new bike."

"Trinity?" Gunner called out when she stopped with her story.

"The party was going great, but I remember I kept looking through the chain-link fence, wondering what was taking him so long. It was at least an hour into the party before my father showed up."

Trinity looked at Gunner and it was as if a fist had tightened around his heart. Seeing her in pain, he wanted to tell her to stop, not to bother to finish the story, but he needed to know. He needed to know what she had against him, against gambling. Tears laced her eyelashes, but none fell.

"I was in the middle of jumping rope, and then I saw him. Oh, my goodness, I was so excited. I took off in a sprint toward my daddy, so happy to finally see him," her voice hitched, "until I realized he was drunk."

"Aw, sweetheart." Gunner started toward her, but stopped when she lifted her hands, palms toward him, forcing him to stop in his tracks. She struggled to keep her tears at bay and he hated she wouldn't let him comfort her. He and his father were very close and Gunner couldn't imagine experiencing something like that.

"I later found out, through hearing him and my mother arguing in their bedroom, that he was supposed to be out buying my birthday gift. The shiny pink bike with the pink-and-white tassels hanging from the handlebars that I'd been begging for. Instead he used the money to gamble, claiming that it wasn't enough for the bike and he knew he could double it."

Gunner went to her. He didn't let the fact that she was backing away stop him this time. He gathered her in his arms and held on, despite her fighting to break loose from his embrace. He didn't let go. After a few minutes, she gave in. She wrapped her arms around his waist and laid her head against his chest, holding him so tightly he could barely breathe.

"I am so sorry for what happened to you," he whispered in her ear. "Now I have a better understanding of why you have a problem with my career." He held her for a few minutes longer, hoping that the closeness offered some comfort. She wasn't crying, but he could feel the tension radiating from her body.

Despite the circumstances, Gunner marveled at how good she felt in his arms. He placed a kiss against her temple, and held her tighter. He could sense the friction between them dissipating and vowed to keep it that way.

Gunner's fresh, clean scent soothed Trinity's anxiety and she snuggled closer, relaxing in his warm embrace. It might not have been the most professional thing to do, but it had been months since she'd had the comfort of a man's strong arms wrapped securely around her. If only she could stay there forever.

As hard as it was to do, Trinity finally pulled out of Gunner's hold, missing his touch the moment she stepped back. She was so ashamed of her behavior and couldn't apologize to him enough for her holier-than-thou attitude. As a woman who had worked in a male-dominant environment for a large part of her life, she knew what it was like for others to criticize or look down on her career choice. So how could she have done the same to him?

"So does this mean that we're calling a truce?" he asked, clearly unwilling to let her go fully, his hand resting on her right hip. "Because I don't want to fight with you…unless we can make up in other ways." He wiggled his eyebrows up and down, his meaning very clear.

Trinity rolled her eyes and laughed, moving a safe distance away, fearing that she'd walk back into his embrace. She appreciated the way he made light of what had just happened. When she looked up at him, he met her gaze, and she didn't miss the concern in his eyes. Each day they spent together, he continued to prove that she had truly misjudged him. Maxwell had been right the day he referred Gunner as a client. It was unfair of her to take her past issues with her father out on Gunner.

"I am so sorry for…everything. I came into your beautiful home, prejudging you and taking my anger toward my father out on you. It is clear that you're very serious about your career and I had no right to say the things I said. Please forgive me."

"Sweetheart, there's nothing to forgive. I'm sorry you went through the things you did with your father, but just remember, I'm not him. It's good we had this fi…discussion. Now I understand a few things about you." He let the back of his hand travel down her cheek and Trinity closed her eyes to his gentle touch. She could feel her defenses weakening whenever she was around him. It didn't help that he was patient, sweet and his touch calming. How was she going to keep her attraction to him under control if he constantly made her feel special and desirable?

She slowly opened her eyes and her gaze met his. It was clear that she wasn't the only one affected by the growing attraction between them. But one of them had to be strong, and she couldn't count on him to be the one.

She backed her way to the door, having a hard time taking her gaze from his. She had dated plenty of great guys and even worked with mostly all men while being a cop, but never had a man affected her the way Gunner had. She wasn't sure what it was about him that made her consider tossing caution out the window, but whatever it was could cause her to make the biggest mistake of her life. She couldn't afford to mess up this assignment, and more important, she couldn't afford to lose her heart to him.

Trinity stood in the middle of the walk-in closet, trying to decide what to wear. Tonight, she and Gunner were going out for dinner, and she wanted to look good, but not like she'd tried too hard. It would help if she knew exactly where they were going, but all he had told her was to dress casually. Everything she brought with her was casual, but considering how frickin' hot it was outside and the fact that she needed to have her weapon on her, that made picking something out a little harder. Besides, it wasn't as if she had a lot of clothes to choose from, so the decision should have been easy. The problem was that going out with Gunner tonight felt more like a date than just an outing. For the past two weeks, they had grown closer and more comfortable with each other and she wanted to wear something drool-worthy.

She pulled out a red sundress that tied at the back of her neck and fit her curves perfectly, stopping at her knees. Tonight she'd just have to carry her handgun in her purse. She grabbed her red strappy sandals and walked out of the closet just as her cell phone rang. Hurrying to her purse that was near the nightstand, she laid the clothes on the bed and snatched up her phone.

"Hello."

"Hey, girl, I'm surprised you answered," Connie said. "I was prepared to leave a message."

"Hey, sis, what's up?" She and Connie were closer than most sisters and Trinity couldn't imagine not having her best friend in her life. "How're things going at the agency? You haven't hit on any of my bodyguards, have you?" she asked, half joking. When it came to men, Connie wasn't shy about showing interest or asking for what she wanted.

"Nah, I told myself that they were off-limits. As for the business, things are going great. That's why I'm calling. Your hunk has referred several people to LEPA and we have five signed contracts just this week."

"Oh, my goodness, that's awesome!" Trinity sat in an upholstered chair near the window and slipped on her shoes. "Are they long-term assignments or short-term?"

"Three are long-term and the other two are short, but have the potential of being long-term."

Connie was a lifesaver. When Trinity agreed to take on the assignment with Gunner, her best friend and assistant was the first person she'd thought of to run the agency while she was away.

"So I'm thinking with all of these referrals, you need to start being a little nice to the hunk."

The better Trinity got to know Gunner, the more she realized that her initial assessment of him was way off. He might still be the arrogant man she knew from back in the day, but she also found that he had a great sense of humor, and was kind and generous. She never asked him for referrals. The fact that he took it upon himself to spread the word about her agency, in such a short time, meant a lot.

"Did you hear me? You need to give the hunk some play."

"Gunner. His name is Gunner."

"Call him what you want, but I will always refer to him as the *hunk*."

Trinity shook her head and smiled. She wouldn't expect anything less from her friend.

"I can't wait to see him again. The next time he's in LA, we should double-date. Oh wait, see if he has a single, *rich*, friend, since I'm single again."

Trinity smiled. Her friend went through men faster than Starbucks went through coffee. "Uh, yeah, okay, I'll see what I can do. But right now I have to go. Gunner's probably waiting for me," Trinity said, giving herself a once-over in the full-length mirror. She had to admit that she looked good, if she could say so herself.

"Another tournament? My goodness, does the man ever take a break?"

Trinity debated whether to tell her friend that Gunner was actually taking her to dinner. Knowing her friend would make more of it than it was, she decided not to tell her.

They talked for a few minutes longer. Connie filled Trinity in on everything else that was going on at the office. There was no way Trinity would have been able to leave her business in anyone else's hands. Despite having some great systems in place, there still needed to be someone overseeing the day-to-day operations.

"Okay, Connie, I really do have to go. Thank you so

much for taking care of my baby for me. I don't know how I would have been able to keep things going at the agency without you."

"Anything for you, sis. And don't forget, be *real* nice to the hunk. If you know what I mean."

Trinity knew exactly what she meant. She also knew that she would never cross that professional line.

Gunner slipped on his suit jacket and bounded down the stairs, keys in hand. He was surprised Trinity agreed to go out to dinner with him, but she quickly reminded him that wherever he went, she went. She was really serious about her bodyguard duties; he could barely take the trash out without her checking the yard first. When she mentioned that she loved Thai food, he knew he had to take her to one of his favorite restaurants.

He stopped short when he entered the kitchen and saw her leaning against the breakfast bar, giving him a front-row view of some of her best assets. Her shapely butt, toned legs that went on forever, and… She stood upright and turned to face him. He had always been a butt man, but with the red halter dress that barely covered her voluptuous breasts, he was quickly changing his mind.

"*Damn*, girl, you definitely don't look like a bodyguard dressed like that. Not that you ever do."

"Well, that's a good thing considering I'm pretending to be your girlfriend," she said, her voice low and sultry. She smiled sweetly. "I guess you like?"

"Heck, yeah, I like." He continued to peruse her attire and stopped at the red sandals that had a wide strap that wrapped around her ankle. The sexy footwear showed off her toes, hosting a hot red nail color. "You did good. You did *very* good," he said, shaking himself out of his trance. "So, are you ready to go?" He could barely take his gaze off her and was starting to wonder if maybe he should have picked a jeans-and-T-shirt place to take her. He quickly squashed the thought. She even made a simple T-shirt and jeans look *hot*.

"Ready when you are." She lifted her handbag from the bar stool and followed him out to the garage. The days that she didn't cook, they'd been either ordering in or picking up meals on the way home. Today he wanted to take her somewhere, hoping that she'd let her guard down so that they could get to know each other better.

Gunner opened the passenger door of his black BMW Alpina Roadster and waited for her to get in, except Trinity hadn't move from her spot near the driver's side door. "What…did you forget something?" he asked.

She held out her hand over the roof of the car. "No, I just need the keys since I'm driving." She narrowed her eyes at him when he looked at her, confused. "You really don't know how this works, do you?"

His thick brows knitted together. "How what works?"

She walked around the vehicle and grabbed hold of the door that he was holding open. "I'm your bodyguard, remember? I'm the one who is trained in defensive driving. Normally, I would insist on my clients riding in the back, but since you only have two-door vehicles, I guess I'll make an exception. Get in."

Gunner shook his head and chuckled. Until now, he had had a driver to transport them to and from the casinos because it was more convenient. So this conversation hadn't come up and actually, he was surprised that it had at all.

He took a step back. "I don't think so, sweetheart. I'm okay with you driving any of these cars—" he gestured to the other two luxury vehicles in the garage "—but I will not be chauffeured around by a woman."

He ignored the way she glared at him and removed her hand from the door.

"Gunner—"

"Trinity, this is not negotiable." He snaked his arm around her tiny waist and backed her against the car. "Yes, I hired you to be my bodyguard and I appreciate how seriously you take your job, but let's get a couple of things straight." He leaned in closer, his thighs touching hers, his hands firmly on her hips. All it would take was for him to move forward an inch, and his lips would be against hers. And if he didn't think she would slug him, that's exactly what he would do.

"I'm a *man* who likes to take the lead, be in control. Besides that, my father would have my head if he knew that I wasn't being a gentleman at all times. That means opening the doors for you, helping you with your chair, and most important, looking out for *your* well-being."

"Gunner, why won't you let me do my job?" she asked softly, the fresh scent of her perfume assaulting his self-control. "Why do you even need me if you're not going to let me do what you're paying me to do?"

This might have started as a business deal, but the more time he spent with her, the more time he wanted to spend with her. He caressed her cheek and stared into her eyes, loving how they held a sparkle that no makeup could improve.

"I didn't survive eighteen years growing up in one of LA's most dangerous neighborhoods to let a woman take care of me. All I need for you to do is be a second set of eyes for me. Basically, watch my back. Understand?"

She huffed and nudged him aside. "You're spending an awful lot of money just to have someone to hang out with. Heck, you could have spent half the amount of money and rented a robo-cop from one of the malls."

He laughed as she climbed into the passenger seat. "Nah, I wanted a professional."

Chapter 9

Trinity glanced around the dimly lit, quaint Thai restaurant, taking in the candlelit walls and the chic decor. A sense of calmness washed over her as she watched the flow of the water and the lily pads floating around in the indoor pond they were sitting next to. The relaxed atmosphere was the perfect way to end the day.

Trinity returned her attention to Gunner. She couldn't get over how good he looked in his dark pinstriped suit and crisp white button-down shirt. He looked more like a confident businessman than a professional poker player. Going tieless, with the top two buttons of his shirt undone, definitely added to his sex appeal. She couldn't help but wonder about the body beneath the clothing. Was it as strong and fit as she imagined? She shook herself to free her mind of imagining him naked. All she knew was that he was a walking billboard for anything tall, dark and sexy.

"So, I'm a little surprised that you remembered the conversation regarding Thai food being my favorite."

"Of course I remember. It was only a couple of weeks ago that you mentioned it."

"But still, I would think that your mind would be clouded with everything poker." Trinity sipped some of her water that the server had left when taking their order.

Gunner chuckled and leaned forward, his arms folded on top of the table. "Trust me. I think about a lot more than just poker." He looked at her pointedly, his friendly brown eyes reflecting a bit of humor.

Fine, I'll play along.

"Like what? What else do you think about besides poker?"

He smiled his charming smile and Trinity couldn't help but smile, too. "Since you knew me back when I was in college, *you're* probably thinking that I only think about partying and women."

Trinity laughed. "Well, yeah. The thought had crossed my mind."

With his gaze lowered, he toyed with the silverware that was on the table near him. "Despite what you might think—" he glanced up at her, all joking aside "—I'm not the young punk kid I used to be. Since graduating from college, I have committed my life to not only playing poker, but giving back."

"How so?" she asked, genuinely interested in what he had to say. Just in the short amount of time she'd been working for him, she could tell he was different, not the same person she remembered.

"Well, for one, I take on numerous philanthropy projects in my old neighborhood and around the world, everything from providing the financing for a new community center to supporting several homeless shelters."

Trinity's heart turned somersaults in her chest. If she could find investors like Gunner to invest in her homeless shelter, she could open it that much sooner. She wanted to say something about her plans, but she didn't want him to think that she had any intention of hitting him up for money—which she didn't.

"Gunner, that's cool and it's something we have in common. I have a soft spot for the homeless population. I support several shelters in LA. But anyway, which is your favorite charity?"

"All right, here you go." Their server seemed to come out of nowhere with their meals. "You had the volcanic chicken—" she put the steaming hot plate down in front of Trinity "—and you had the nut-crusted salmon," she said to Gunner. "Is there anything else I can get you?"

Trinity almost laughed aloud at how hard the girl was cheesing at Gunner. And as usual, he seemed totally oblivious of the attention he often received from women.

Gunner glanced at his food and shook his head. "No, I think everything looks great. What about you? Need anything else?" Gunner asked. Trinity didn't miss how his gaze traveled down her body every time he looked at her. She had paid a small fortune for the Vera Wang halter dress and the admiration she saw in his eyes made it all worth it.

"Nope, I think I'm good."

They both tasted their food and Trinity closed her

eyes, savoring the spicy chicken. She could eat Thai food every day; the hotter the dish, the better.

"Good, huh?" Gunner asked, grinning at her. "I love watching you eat. The way you appreciate each bite and the little moan…" He stopped and laughed when she cocked an eyebrow at him. "Anyway, what I'm trying to say, you definitely seem to enjoy your meals."

"You mean I'm greedy." She laughed.

He shook his head vehemently, still grinning. "No, that's not what I meant at all. I love to eat and it's nice to be with a woman who doesn't pick over her food." He wiped his mouth. "Anyway, let's change the subject before I get myself into trouble."

"Good idea. So, getting back to our conversation."

"Oh, yeah, you were asking which is my favorite charity." He twirled the soba noodles around on his fork and lifted it to his mouth, but stopped. "Wait, you said we have something in common—supporting the homeless. Are they your favorite cause because of your childhood?"

"Partly, but during my time as a cop, I worked in an area that had a high homeless population." She sighed, thinking about her peeps, especially Lucy. She couldn't discuss the homeless without them coming to mind. "I know there will always be people who are less fortunate than us, but it bothers me that this country still has people living on the streets."

"Yeah, I know what you mean. When I first started making money, it took me a while to feel comfortable spending it." He laughed when she made a face. Trinity found it hard to believe that anyone would have trouble spending millions. "I'm serious. Granted, I invest a lot of time into my career and work hard for my money, but it did take me a while to get over the…I don't know, guilt, I guess. Here I was, making all of this money, and there were people who barely had a hot meal every day."

Trinity nodded. She had never thought about that side of being wealthy and wondered what she would do if she suddenly came into a lot of cash. With all of the needs in the world, she would never have enough to support every organization that she would probably want to support.

"Going back to my other question, which is your favorite organization that you support?"

Gunner wiped his mouth. "I would have to say On Time Missionary Group. My mother, who is a missionary, started it years ago. They do some amazing work. In the past two years, they've been to four different developing nations. Most of the missionaries in the group are nurses. The organization provides medical support of all kinds. Their focus lately has been on countries that have endured things like earthquakes, tsunamis and other natural disasters."

Again, Trinity's mind went to Lucy. She'd heard from Jesse, who said that her peeps were fine. Unfortunately his brother, the doctor, hadn't been able to go out there with him that day.

"I think people who have a heart to volunteer their time like that, especially in emerging countries, are amazing," Trinity said. "Though I've done some volunteer work, I don't know if I'm compassionate enough for *that* type of work."

"You don't think so?"

She shook her head and wiped her mouth with the cloth napkin. "Nah. You really have to be a people person and I'm more of a task-oriented person. What about you?"

"I'm not like my mother. When my sisters and I were growing up, she always talked about going to other countries and doing missionary work. She has always loved helping people. I've gone on a couple of trips with her, but it was too depressing. No matter how much money I donate, it will never be enough. It's hard to see such devastation." He shook his head and Trinity could feel the compassion he had for those less fortunate.

She placed her elbow on the table and rested her chin in her hand. Despite his net worth, Gunner had to be one of the most laid-back people she had ever known. No one would ever suspect he was worth millions. Though he was paying her a small fortune to *watch his back*, she never would have guessed him to be as generous as she'd seen him be over the last couple of weeks. With every meal, he gave huge tips, whether food was delivered or whether they were picking up their meals. The other day, he had received a large package and when she asked about it, he told her it was a thank-you gift from one of his parents' friends. Gunner had covered their son's medical expenses when he found out the guy's insurance would only pay half the cost. Then there was her and her agency. For him to pay triple her fee, she was pretty sure Max had probably told him about her tax situation. Normally she would be upset that her brother shared her personal business, but these days she needed all the financial assistance she could get.

"So are you enjoying your meal?" Gunner asked, shoving a forkful of salmon into his mouth.

"Are you kidding? I see why this is one of your favorite restaurants. The food is outstanding. Thank you for bringing me, even though you didn't have to."

"It was the least I could do, considering the meals you've been preparing. Besides, you've been a trouper, traveling around with me and hitting these tournaments."

She almost reminded him that he was paying her good money to go wherever he went, but thought better of it and kept her mouth shut.

"We'll be heading to New Orleans the day after tomorrow."

"How long will we be there?"

He had just put food into his mouth before she'd posed the question. She watched him chew, unable to take her gaze from the way his alluring lips moved.

"Four days," he finally responded.

They ate and talked and Trinity found herself getting more and more interested in all that went into the various poker tours and the PPO.

"So, help me to understand. If you have already qualified to participate in the PPO this summer, why partake in all of these other tournaments? Shouldn't you be getting mentally prepared, or resting up for the Main Event?"

Gunner swirled the straw around in his glass, ice knocking together noisily, while deep in thought. "I love the game," he finally said. Trinity couldn't help but notice the way his eyes lit up when he talked about poker. She was sorry she had ever compared Gunner to her father.

"I won't be playing all the time at some of the tournament events. In some cases, I agreed to attend because the host casinos have invited me. For instance, we'll be traveling to Florida, all expenses paid, for a regional event, but I won't be participating in the tournament. I'll just be hanging out for publicity's sake, and maybe play a little at one of the casino tables. Either way, it'll be the last event we'll attend until the PPO, which begins after Memorial Day."

Trinity shook her head. "I don't know how you keep it all straight or even how you physically keep up. All of the traveling has to be exhausting."

"It used to be when I first started years ago, trying to work my way up as one of the best players in the world," he said without sounding cocky.

"Did you play poker in college? Was this something you always wanted to do?"

He chuckled and shook his head. "As a kid, my grandfather taught me how to play and we played often. And no, it wasn't something I always wanted to do. I actually went to school for accounting."

Trinity's mouth dropped open. "An accountant? You wanted to be an accountant. I would have never guessed." Somehow, she couldn't picture him sitting in a stuffy office, with a pencil behind his ear, crunching numbers all day long. Although...if she had an accountant who looked like Gunner, she would find all types of reasons to go and see him.

"I love math," Gunner said. "That's probably why I do well with poker."

They ate and continued to talk about everything from tournaments to the different variations of poker. The more time she spent with him, the more comfortable she felt.

"Maybe you can teach me how to play poker some-time," Trinity said, finishing off her meal.

"I would love to teach you how to play. Maybe we can start tonight."

Hours later, they sat in Gunner's game room at one of the poker tables. Gunner had no idea he would enjoy teaching anyone the game this much. Most women he had dated couldn't care less about the game of poker. They were more interested in his winnings and being seen on his arm. The idea of sharing something he loved with a woman that he was very much interested in was a serious turn-on.

"Wait a minute. I have two aces, a king, a queen and a jack. How did you beat my hand with twos, threes and a four?" she asked, sounding defeated. "I thought with all of these high cards, I'd win this hand."

He shook his head. "Not in this case. I have two pairs—the two twos, and two threes. It's considered the lowest-valued hand, but it beats yours because you only have one pair and that's the aces. The high cards in your hand don't help you in this case."

Trinity tossed the cards on the table and dropped her head back, covering her eyes with her hands. "I think my brain is going to explode. How in the world do you keep all of this straight?" She sat up and dropped her hands onto the table. "I don't think I'm ever going to learn this stuff." She looked at him with those big brown eyes and pouty lips. Gunner didn't know how it was possible, but she seemed to get prettier by the day.

"Sweetheart, you've only been doing this for a cou-ple of hours. It has taken me *years* to learn the game. Don't be so hard on yourself."

"Yeah, I guess." Her hand covered her mouth to hide a yawn. "One thing's for sure, I can see why you enjoy playing. I don't even know what I'm doing, yet I'm looking forward to playing again."

"I'm glad to hear that. You're a fast learner and I'm going to enjoy teaching you everything I know."

Trinity raised an arched eyebrow and looked at him suspiciously.

"What?" Gunner shrugged and feigned innocence with his comment and its double meaning. "I just want to make sure you're well prepared for—"

She lifted her hand. "You might as well stop while you're ahead before you say anything more and have me throwing something at you," she joked.

Gunner laughed. They were definitely more comfortable with each other and he was looking forward to seeing where their newfound camaraderie took them. When he invited her out for dinner, he hadn't called it a date, but in his mind, it was their first date. He had to admit that he was looking forward to spending more time with his beautiful bodyguard.

Trinity lifted her arms above her head and stretched. She had changed into a blue tank top and a pair of denim shorts that showed off just how fit she was. Since arriving in Vegas, Gunner had only known her to work out a couple of times, and most of those times she had been doing yoga. How she kept everything tight in all the right places was a mystery to him.

"All right, I think I'm going to have to call it a night." She stood and adjusted her shirt. "Thanks for tonight. I had a really good time."

"Me, too." Gunner followed her out of the game room and up the stairs. He glanced at his watch; it was two in the morning. He often lost track of time when playing poker or entertaining a gorgeous woman. In this case, he was doubly distracted.

They stopped near her bedroom door.

"So when can you teach me more?"

He stepped closer to her, causing her to take a step back, but the wall kept her from retreating any farther.

"Any time you want." He placed his hands on the wall on each side of her head, blocking her in. "You just say when." His mouth was mere inches from her lips as he gazed into her eyes. When he leaned in more, she stiffened and it took herculean strength to not cover her mouth with his and become reacquainted with her sweet lips. Instead of doing what he really wanted to do, he placed a lingering kiss against her cheek and backed away. He had vowed that the next time he kissed her, she wouldn't want to push him away. It was a good thing he was a patient man.

"Have a good night," he said and turned in the direction of his bedroom. *It's going to be a long one.*

Chapter 10

Gunner glanced at the clock. *Five-fifteen in the morning.* He had only slept for three hours and for whatever reason, he couldn't fall back to sleep. Thoughts of Trinity and their first date infiltrated his mind. He'd had more sleepless nights since she'd been under his roof than he cared to count. Last night, or better yet this morning, had been the worst. The long, cold shower he had taken when he retired to his room did nothing to tame the fire that she had stoked within his body. Her sexy outfits, her womanly curves and everything else about her were wreaking havoc on his self-control.

I might as well get up.

He slipped into his briefs and reached for his phone. It was really too early to be calling anyone, but he dialed anyway. For the past three years, it had been tradition for him to call his father on this day.

"I was wondering when I'd hear from you," his father said after answering the phone on the first ring.

"Hey, Pops. Did I wake you?" Gunner fluffed his pillow and lay back on the bed. His brain was awake, but his body was wound tight. "So how's the family? Have my niece and nephew worn you out yet?"

His father had retired earlier in the year and had volunteered to help Gunner's sister around the house when her husband was deployed to Afghanistan.

"They're great kids. I can't believe how big they're getting and how smart they are. Brina has been helping me learn how to use my new laptop, and Sam is going to be the next Aníbal Sánchez. That kid has a serious arm on him and lives and breathes baseball."

Gunner smiled. "You definitely sound like a proud grandpa."

Silence fell between them before his father spoke. "*Your* grandpa would have been seventy-five today. I sure do miss that old man."

"Yeah, me, too," Gunner said, his voice heavy with emotion. It had been three years since his grandfather passed away from pancreatic cancer. The cancer had gone into remission for a number of years, then came back with a vengeance, taking his grandfather's life within months. There wasn't a day that went by that Gunner didn't think about him, especially during this time of the year. He had been Gunner's biggest fan and the one who spearheaded his career.

"Dad would have been so proud of the man you have become. Like I am. I know I don't tell you this often, but I am so proud of you, son."

"Thanks, Pop, the feelings are mutual." Growing up, their family didn't have much, but there was no doubt that his parents loved him and his two sisters. "So have you talked to Mom lately?" His parents divorced a couple of years after Gunner's youngest sister moved out. Unlike many other divorced couples, his parents were still the best of friends.

"Actually, I talked with her yesterday and she's well. She's still enjoying her missionary work in Haiti." After the divorce, his mother pursued her life-long desire to travel the world and help people who were in need. Gunner's father and sisters weren't too happy with her decision, but Gunner supported the life change, encouraging her to do it while she was still able.

Gunner slipped into his running clothes while he and his father talked for a few minutes longer.

"Okay, Pop, I'm going to head out for a run, but I'll talk to you soon."

Gunner finished dressing, grabbed his keys and fifteen minutes later, he was hitting the pavement. He hated leaving without letting Trinity know, but he had been itching for a run for the past couple of days and today was the perfect day to get out. He always got like this on his grandfather's birthday, as well as the anniversary of his death. Besides, she would have insisted on going with him and he needed some time to himself, and some time away from her.

Who wouldn't miss the man? He had been Gunner's confidant, his mentor and the person who had bankrolled his first poker tournament.

A smile found its way to Gunner's lips as he glanced over his shoulder to check for oncoming traffic before crossing the busy street. A warm feeling of gratitude washed over him whenever he thought about all the good times he and his grandfather had together. His grandfather had taught him everything from fishing to how to change the oil in his car. Most important, he had taught him the game of poker. Before Gunner went off to college, very few weekends passed that they didn't play Texas hold 'em or five-card stud. It was both of their favorite pastimes. After Gunner graduated, he had looked into playing in his first live poker tournament, only to find out that it would cost ten thousand dollars to participate. His grandfather fronted the cost and it turned out to be the event that had jump-started Gunner's career.

Gunner looked up and realized he had run a lot farther than planned. The sun had made its ascent, and there were a few more cars on the road. He turned to run back the way he came, but slowed again when an eerie sensation crept up his spine. *What the hell?*

He glanced back, but didn't see anything suspicious or anyone following him. He shook his head and chuckled. Apparently, Trinity's overprotection and the crap involving his poker-playing opponents were making him paranoid. *All right, man; don't go getting all soft.*

Gunner approached a stoplight and slowed, but continued to jog in place. Using his forearm to wipe the perspiration from his forehead, he blew out a couple of breaths. He needed to pick up his pace. Otherwise, Trinity would be awake and he would never hear the end of it from her. Not only that, it was at least eighty degrees and he felt like he was jogging inside of a sauna.

The light changed to green and the same eerie sensation returned. Gunner glanced over his shoulder. A dark sedan with tinted windows crept down the street, but he didn't think much of it. People got lost in the area all the time.

He turned at the next corner and nodded as he passed a couple of women pushing baby strollers. Seeing them made him think about the family he hoped to have someday. On his next birthday, he would be thirty-one, and he was finally ready to settle down. Trinity immediately came to mind. This was the first time in his life that he could actually envision sharing his life with a specific woman without it freaking him out.

"Look out!" someone yelled.

Gunner glanced back in time to see the dark sedan speeding in his direction.

Damn.

He kicked his legs and pumped his arms as they propelled him forward, but not fast enough. The car closed in on him. Panic rioted through him; his heart hammered loudly in his chest and sweat dripped into his eyes. He ran faster, pushing himself harder, trying to put some distance between him and the vehicle. Just as he cut across a corner lot, the car jumped the curb. He couldn't get out of the way fast enough. The car nipped the side of his body. A guttural howl like that of a wounded bear started in his gut and shot out of his mouth. His body went sailing through the air before crashing into some bushes, a searing pain shooting through his side.

The other vehicle sped off and, before Gunner could catch his breath, a small crowd of people surrounded him.

"Are you okay?"

"Somebody call 911."

"Stop! Don't move him."

Everyone spoke at once and the constant chatter slowly drifted to the background. Gunner squeezed his eyes shut and gritted his teeth against the throbbing in his leg and hip, trying unsuccessfully to relax his muscles and catch his breath. After a few deep breaths, he sent up a quick prayer of thanks. At least he was alive.

His next thoughts were filled with thoughts of Trinity. *She's going to kill me.*

"I am going to kill him," Trinity seethed when she checked the three-car garage to see if any of Gunner's vehicles were missing. She had scoured the place up and down in search of him, hoping that he hadn't left the house as she suspected. *This is ridiculous! How am I supposed to guard someone who refuses to follow my rules?*

She stepped outside and into the backyard. She was pretty sure he wasn't out there, but it had been the only place she hadn't checked. *Where is he?* Anger had been the dominant emotion when she first suspected he wasn't there, but worry was starting to settle into her bones.

Trinity marched back into the house and locked the sliding glass door behind her. She dialed Gunner's cell phone again, and again it went to voice mail.

"Damn him!" She paced in front of the kitchen counter, wondering where he'd gone. She didn't know if he had called a driver or if he was somewhere on foot.

She jumped when her cell phone rang. "Gunner!" she answered on the first ring. Silence greeted her on the other end before anyone spoke.

"Nope, it's me," her brother, Maxwell, said. "Why

would you be thinking it was Gunner calling when you're supposed to be guarding him?"

"Because the stupid jerk snuck out of the house this morning without telling me." She couldn't believe that she hadn't heard the door chime.

Irritation singed every nerve ending within her and she clenched her jaw shut to keep from spewing the curse words that were dangling on the tip of her tongue.

"How could you misplace your client so early in the morning? It's not even seven o'clock yet and, knowing Gunner, if he had a tournament last night, you guys probably didn't get in before two or three. Are you sure he came home with you last night?"

Trinity ignored the humor in her brother's tone and sucked in a calming breath before she spoke. "Max, do you happen to know where he is?"

"Nah, I haven't talked to him in a couple of days. I was actually calling to see how you two were making out."

Heat rose to Trinity's face when she thought about the kiss she and Gunner had shared. If her brother knew she had made out with her client, she would never hear the end of it, especially since said client was his best friend.

She cleared her throat. "We were making out just fine until this little stunt." She returned to pacing the length of the kitchen. "I was planning to call you later today anyway. Do you guys have any suspects in connection to the incidents with the three poker players? Any witnesses, clues, anything?"

"We've talked to a few people of interest and a couple of witnesses from the first two incidents. Unfortunately, there's nothing to suggest that the attacks are connected."

Trinity cursed under her breath. She was starting to think that Gunner was right, that the incidents were connected.

"Well, keep me posted if you find out anything."

"Will do. Call me back if Gunner doesn't check in soon. He might be out jogging."

An hour later, Trinity was in the kitchen wiping down the counters when the house alarm went off. Removing her small pistol from her ankle holster, she eased around the corner and into the hallway.

"I ought to shoot you just for the hell of it," she said from the far end of the hallway when Gunner walked into the house. "You hired me to watch your back. How am I supposed to do that when you leave the house without telling me?"

"Trinity," he breathed.

She holstered her gun and folded her arms across her chest, waiting for him to say more. When he didn't, another smart remark teetered on the tip of her tongue, but then she noticed he hadn't moved. "Gunner...what's wrong?" A wave of apprehension swept through her as she eased toward him. The closer she got, the more closely her gaze traveled the length of his body. "Oh, my God! What happened?" She didn't miss the pain etched on his face, the bandage on the side of his temple and the ripped pants.

"Someone ran me off the road."

"What? When? How?" she rattled off, barely taking a breath. "Tell me what happened."

Trinity led him toward the kitchen, ducking in the powder room for a hand towel along the way. Gunner sat on one of the bar stools and she noticed the slowness of his moves.

"Gunner," she said, wetting the towel and then walking over to him. "We should get you to a hospital to have you checked out. A blood stain has seeped through the bandage on the side of your head."

He started to shake his head, but stopped as if he were in pain. "No. Paramedics checked me out already."

"And they didn't take you to the hospital?" She stepped back, the anger from earlier returning. "What is wrong with them? You need to be checked out."

"I refused. Told them I was fine," he said in a monotone voice.

"You don't look fine. I can't believe they didn't insist." She dabbed at a few scratches on the side of his face and he flinched, glaring at her.

"I'm sorry. Tell me what happened."

Gunner told her about his run and the eerie feeling of being followed. "When I looked back again, the car was barreling toward me." He shrugged. "I couldn't get out of the way fast enough. The car clipped my side and I landed on my right hip near some bushes."

"Were you able to get a look at the driver? Did anyone get the license plate, a description of the car or anything?"

"Everything happened so fast. All I know is that it was a dark sedan with tinted windows. No plates."

Anger crawled through Trinity's veins. "See, if you hadn't snuck out of the house, this probably wouldn't have happened!" She pointed her finger at him, jerking it back and forth with every word. "When are you going to understand how this bodyguard thing works?

You are not to go *anywhere*, and I mean *anywhere*, without me. Got it?"

Seconds passed as she glared at him and he stared back at her without speaking, his eyes focused on her lips. Trinity stepped back, ensuring that he wouldn't suddenly kiss her the way he had before. She'd be lying if she said that she hadn't enjoyed it, but there was no way she was letting it happened again.

"Gunner—"

"I heard you, Trinity," he said with attitude. "I'm not to go anywhere without you." He stood slowly, cursing with every move he made. Why he was being so stubborn about going to the hospital, she wasn't sure. He could barely walk.

"Maybe you can get cleaned up in the bathroom down here so you won't have to tackle the stairs."

He stopped, cursed and held his side before he began moving again.

"I really think you should—"

"Forget it, Trinity. I'm not going to the hospital." He walked slowly out of the kitchen with her following close behind. "All I need is a long soak in my tub and maybe a stiff drink."

"But I thought you didn't drink." She almost bumped into him when he stopped suddenly. According to him, he had consumed enough alcohol while in college to last a lifetime.

"I don't, but I could use one."

"I can't believe you can joke considering what you've just gone through. Do you need me to help you up the stairs?" She stood next to him, her hand on his lower back.

He shook his head. "I think I can make it."

"Then what can I do to help?" If she couldn't talk him into going to the hospital and getting checked out, she wanted to do whatever she could to make him feel better.

"You can come upstairs with me and wash my back."

She heard the humor in his voice and narrowed her eyes at him, her hands on her hips. "That's not going to happen. So try again. What can I do to help you?"

He brushed a lock of hair from her face and pushed it behind her ear, something she did often. Seconds passed before he spoke.

"Find the bastard who tried to kill me."

Gunner stepped out of the Jacuzzi tub and wrapped a towel around his waist, feeling better than he had a half an hour earlier. He looked at himself in the mirror. He removed the bloody bandage from over his right temple and examined the cut that looked worse than it felt. His mother always said he had a hard head. Today proved her right. The bruise on his legs and hip would probably linger for a couple of weeks, but the mental images that kept flashing before his eyes were going to be a different story. He couldn't shake the fear of seeing that car plowing toward him with every intent of killing him. He had no idea who would hate him enough to come after him. But when he got his hands on the person behind all of this, he was going to make them sorry they ever targeted poker players.

Trinity balanced the tray of food with her left hand and knocked on Gunner's bedroom door with the other. She figured he'd probably be hungry and had made him a sandwich and added some pasta salad that was leftover from the day before. Knocking again without getting an answer, she wondered if he'd fallen asleep.

She opened his door slightly and called out to him with still no answer. Stepping inside, she glanced around the huge space and walked farther in when she didn't see him. *He must still be in the bathtub.* She placed the tray in the sitting area on the mosaic table that was in front of the love seat. He would see it the moment he came out of the bathroom.

Just as she turned to leave the room, the bathroom door opened.

Oh. My. God. Trinity stood frozen in place, her pulse pounding in her ear, heat rushing through her veins. In all of her twenty-eight years, never had she seen a more magnificent sight than the naked man standing before her. When God was handing out body parts, he clearly saved his best for Gunner.

She finally released the breath that was lodged within her, but couldn't divert her gaze from the perfection standing only six feet away. A muscular chest and broad shoulders that tapered down to flat abs— she couldn't believe he'd been hiding such flawlessness beneath his T-shirt and worn jeans. And with the thick package he was working with, it was no wonder women vied for his attention back in college. A body like his should be showcased for the world to see, or for at least every woman with a pulse.

"I guess if you're going to guard my body, you might as well see what you're guarding." He eased across the room as if walking around naked in front of her was the most natural thing to do.

At his dresser, he pulled an item from the top drawer

and stepped into a pair of sleek black boxer briefs. When he turned and faced her, Trinity's heart fluttered wildly and a wave of dizziness draped over her like a heavy quilt. Her hand flew to her chest and she leaned against the side of a chair in his sitting room to catch her breath. She couldn't stop her gaze from zeroing in on his semi-erection pressed firmly against his briefs. His thick, tree-trunk legs were spread apart as if making sure she got a good look. Gunner in sexy underwear was just as enticing as him naked.

"Trinity?" Gunner's deep, hypnotic voice called out. "You okay?"

Her gaze met his, but jockeyed back and forth from his eyes to his penis that was struggling to break free. She swallowed, feeling as if she was slowly coming back to herself. But then…he adjusted himself.

Ohmygod, ohmygod, ohmygod. She diverted her eyes. *I have to get out of here before I do something I'll regret.*

"Uh…" She glanced at him again and pointed to the meal she had brought upstairs, "food…eat," she stuttered, not missing the amusement in his eyes. She slowly backed away on shaky legs, unable to pull her gaze from his tempting body. It wasn't until she bumped into the wall that she snapped out of the fog she'd been in. She quickly left the room, slamming the door behind her.

Gunner's laughter followed her down the hall and she knew she would never be able to look at him the same way again.

Damn him.

Moments later, behind the safety of her bedroom door, she collapsed on top of the bed, staring up at the ceiling. *I'm in so much trouble. I can't do this. I can't stay with him.* Visions of his hard, naked body assaulted her senses and she squeezed her thighs together, trying to stop the throbbing between her legs. A whimper escaped her lips when she drew her knees to her chest and wrapped her arms around her legs. Squeezing. Deep breathing. Nothing worked.

She bolted up into a sitting position. "Okay, Trinity, calm down. Breathe. That's it, just breathe." She coached herself, repeating the words over and over aloud. When her pounding pulse slowed, she took several more cleansing breaths and then reached for her cell phone. She did what any woman on the verge of jumping off a cliff would do. She called her best friend.

After several rings, Connie picked up.

"Hey, girl. I was just thinking about you, wondering when you were going to call me. Tell me, how are things going with the hunk? Why—"

"I think I'm in trouble," Trinity whispered, not missing the trembling in her own voice.

"Oh, my God! What? Where are you? Are you hurt?" her friend asked, her voice frantic. Trinity cursed under her breath, forgetting how quickly Connie jumped to conclusions. "Trinity, what happened?"

"Connie?" Trinity called out several times before her friend calmed down. "I'm okay…well, at least physically."

"What? You scared me half to death. I thought you'd been shot or something. Don't you ever do that to me again!" she fussed.

"I think I'm falling for my client," Trinity said, knowing that would shut her friend up. Silence filled the phone line before Connie screamed into the phone.

Trinity pulled it away from her ear, imagining her friend doing one of her stupid happy dances.

"Tell me everything," she finally said. "And I mean everything. You know I'm not like others who might want you to leave out the juicy stuff. I want to know it all. Speak!"

Trinity rolled her eyes. "I only have a few minutes, but...but we kissed..." Another scream erupted from her friend and Trinity was starting to think that maybe it had been a bad idea to call her. "Would you calm down?"

"Okay, okay, I'm sorry. Keep going."

Trinity told her about the sexual tension brewing between them. It took her a while to calm her friend down when she explained how an offer to teach Gunner some self-defense moves turned into a heated kiss.

"I knew it. I knew it. There was no way that nothing could be going on between you and the hunk."

Trinity didn't bother commenting on the nickname that Connie had given Gunner. "What made you think anything would be going on with me and the hu... Gunner?"

"Don't think I didn't hear that near slipup." Her friend laughed. "But I won't go there. Let's just say that I've seen the *hunk*. If nothing were happening between you two, living in close quarters and him being as gorgeous as he is, then I would think something was wrong with you. I'm sorry, but a man that fine should not be wasted."

"You know good and well I can't cross that line with Gunner. He's a client!"

"But he's a man first and apparently he's interested."

"I have to admit, Connie. I'm scared. I'm scared

I'm going to ruin this business deal because I'm so attracted to him. And the worst part is—I like him." Trinity felt sick. She couldn't believe they were even having this conversation. And more important, she couldn't believe that she was thinking about forgoing all professionalism to be with Gunner.

"Finally! I'm glad you're finally admitting that you like him."

"You act as if that's a good thing! We leave for New Orleans in a couple of days. What if—"

"Girl, just go with it. Quit being such a goody-goody."

"Connie, I can't. We need this contract."

"Yes, you can. You deserve to let your hair down for a change and get your freak on! Besides, you've already cashed his check. I say, get yours, girl!"

Chapter 11

"Looks as if you had a good run this evening," a reporter said to Gunner when he stepped away from a poker table. Instead of participating in the tournament, he played a few cash games, walking away with three times as much as he started with. This was his and Trinity's last day in New Orleans and he was more than ready to go home. "I take it that Roman Jeers's trash talking didn't distract you," the woman stated, more than asked, before turning the mic to him.

"Not really," Gunner replied absently, having a hard time keeping his gaze from lingering on Trinity. He'd spotted a poker player, Simon McCallum, earlier, trying to talk to her, and it looked as if he had returned. "I've played at the same table with Roman on a number of occasions and if nothing else, he's consistent with his excessive talking."

With the huge crowd of people standing near the

entrance to the card room, Gunner had to lean closer to the woman, talking louder than usual. He answered a few more questions, then excused himself. He kept his gaze on Trinity and her admirer as he approached, getting more pissed the closer he got. Trinity was a beautiful woman, but he didn't think he'd ever get used to men gawking at her. Normally he wasn't the jealous type, but damn if he didn't want to put a glass box around her and shut out all of her admirers. It was way past time he staked his claim.

Just before he reached her, she glanced up. Gunner wasn't sure what he saw in his face, but when her gaze met his, she took a step away from her visitor.

"Hey, sweetheart." Gunner slid a possessive arm around her narrow waist, his hand resting on her hip. Before she could react to his touch, he lowered his mouth over hers and the intoxicating scent of her perfume washed over him like a cool, gentle breeze. Lips so soft and sweet connected with his and he temporarily forgot that he was only trying to get rid of her admirer. Suddenly not caring who was watching, he tightened his grip around her waist and placed his other hand behind her head, pulling her closer, securing their bodies together. At this moment, nothing else mattered to him. He didn't care that he had barely slept for the past three days because sharing a hotel suite with Trinity and not being able to touch her was too much. But tonight—tonight would be different.

Gunner's heart lurched when Trinity moaned and wrapped her arm around his neck, pressing her soft curves against the hardness of his body, and deepening the kiss. She kissed him with reckless abandonment and he knew that tonight she would be his. He had been with plenty of women, but there were none that he wanted as badly as he wanted her. He didn't normally participate in public displays of affection, but he wanted everyone to know that she was with him. With the way she was kissing him, she had just raised the stakes and there was no turning back.

"Excuse me, Mr. Brooks, who's the lovely lady?"

"Is there wedding news to share?"

Gunner reluctantly ended the kiss when question after question from reporters bombarded him, yet he didn't release Trinity. He couldn't. Now that he had her in his arms, he never wanted to let her go.

"Wow," Trinity mumbled, her fingers touching her lips as she stared up at him shyly.

Gunner kept his arm around her and turned his back to a couple of reporters. "'Wow' is right." He placed a kiss against her temple. "You okay?" She nodded.

He ran his hands up and down her side, shocked that she hadn't tackled him to the floor and maybe handcuffed him for kissing her. Or at the very least cursed him out. He wanted nothing more than to carry her out of there and go straight to their suite to finish what they both so clearly wanted. Unfortunately, he had promised a reporter friend of his a brief interview in the media room.

Holding Trinity close to his side, Gunner ignored the curious stares and the questions still being tossed at him, but he hadn't forgotten about her admirer. Turning back, he noticed Simon had stepped off to the side, his gaze still on Trinity.

With Trinity in tow, Gunner walked in Simon's direction, making sure the man was close enough to hear what he had to say.

"Stay the hell away from her," Gunner said in a low, lethal voice. He didn't stick around for a response; instead he guided Trinity out into the hall. Before they could get too far, they were stopped by yet another reporter. Gunner already didn't enjoy talking to the media and he liked it even less now that they were asking questions about him and Trinity.

Trinity's lips were still warm and moist from Gunner's surprise kiss as she allowed him to lead her out of the card room. She didn't know what the kiss was about, but Lord knows she didn't want it to end.

So much for professionalism.

For the past few days, he had guided her around as if they were more than business associates, making it too easy for her to fall into the role of girlfriend. Since their dinner a week earlier, things between them had definitely changed. Connie's words rattled around in her head and Trinity was starting to think that maybe her friend was right. Maybe it was time for her to let loose and accept the inevitable. Fate had brought her and Gunner together and God knows she wanted him.

"Let me talk to this reporter and then we can head back to the suite," Gunner said against her ear, giving her a gentle squeeze before removing his arm from around her waist. "You'll be okay?"

Trinity almost laughed. He so didn't understand how this bodyguard thing worked. Considering the butterflies floating around her stomach and the way her body was responding to his nearness, apparently she didn't, either.

I need to get a grip.

After assuring Gunner that she could take care of

herself if any other unwanted admirers approached her, she took a couple of steps back. Observing him being interviewed by an ESPN reporter, she would have to agree with Connie. Gunner was a hunk. Sexy without even trying. At six-one, he had the smoothest dark skin she had ever seen on a man, and those eyes, those intense eyes that glanced her way every couple of minutes, made her feel not only cherished, but desired. And for the second time, she'd had an opportunity to taste those full, sensual lips. Everything about him oozed sex appeal. He was gorgeous in college, but tonight Trinity was seeing him in a different light. For the first time since meeting him years ago, she saw the man he was on the inside—the laid-back, funny, generous man who lived a rich, yet simple, life.

"That was quite a show you and Brooks put on back there." Trinity turned to find the guy from earlier standing a little too close and gazing at her as if she were going to be his last supper. She remembered him from a tournament a few weeks ago. He was the one with the shiny keychain, the brass owl. "Was that for my benefit?"

"Listen," she began, "I have already told you that I'm not interested. What's it going to take for you to move on and stay away from me?" Trinity had dealt with plenty of jerks like him while working for the LAPD, but what she didn't want to do was make a scene. She hoped that talking to him would get him to move on. Instead, he moved in closer, his offensive breath smelling of liquor. Trinity gave him a once-over. He really wasn't a bad-looking guy. His skin was the color of mocha; light brown eyes and wavy black hair accented his full face. He smiled, revealing a dimple in his left cheek. Actually, he was quite handsome. She just wasn't interested.

"Why don't you let me kiss you? I'm sure I can top that punk-ass kiss Brooks planted on you."

He placed his hands on her arm and instinctively, Trinity grabbed his wrist. She twisted her body, and flipped him to the floor. A loud thud caught the attention of a few. Not wanting to draw any more attention, she moved away.

"Why, you little bi—" He jumped up and charged toward her.

"I told your ass to stay the hell away from her!" Gunner growled. He grabbed Simon by his shirt and slammed him against the wall.

"Oh, no. Gunner!"

Trinity tried to pull him away before he did something he would regret. Camera flashes temporarily blinded her and she moved to the other side of Gunner, hoping to block him from any other photos. She wanted to step in and take over, but she remembered the speech that Gunner had given her about him being a man. She definitely didn't want to do anything that would make him feel like less than a man, but...

"Gunner, let's just go. Security is headed this way."

The reporter he'd been talking to, as well as a few others, crowded around, hoping to get a big scoop.

"Come near her again and I won't be responsible for what I do to you." There was a lethal edge to his words, which caught Trinity by surprise.

"Babe, please, you're making a scene," she reasoned. "Let's just go. He's not worth it."

Gunner scanned her from head to toe, still not releasing the man. "Are you okay?" His voice was low and raspy, his eyes sharp and assessing. Both were doing wicked things to her. She was attracted to the quiet, unpretentious side of him, but this side of him was a serious turn-on. So used to being independent and the one who usually took out the bad guy, it was refreshing to feel like the damsel in distress for a change.

"I'm fine. Just release him." She yanked on Gunner's arm, feeling his muscles contract beneath her touch. He didn't let go of the man. "Gunner...please."

Gunner gave the man one more glare before he released him and turned to Trinity. "Let's get out of here."

Gunner made eye contact with security, but said nothing; only a head nod was exchanged. Trinity didn't know if that was some type of secret language, but whatever it was, security didn't stop them. Gunner had a tight grip on her hand and pushed his way through the small crowd that had formed, again ignoring questions thrown at him.

"All right, nothing to see here," Trinity heard the security guard say as Gunner hurried them away.

Too shocked to say anything, Trinity allowed him to hasten her to the elevator. She didn't speak until they were safely onboard.

"You really don't get this whole bodyguard thing, do you?" she said to lighten the mood. She stood in front of him, but he kept his attention on the numbers above the door. "I can't believe you'd risk your reputation and...and your life tussling with some jerk. He could have had a knife or anything. Then where would that have left you with regard to the PPO? When are you going to let me do my job?"

The elevator doors opened on their floor and Gunner still hadn't spoken. He grabbed hold of her elbow and pulled her in the direction of their suite. It wasn't until they walked into the room and closed the door that he exploded.

"What the hell was going on with you and Simon?" he yelled. "Why were you entertaining anything he had to say?"

"Me?" She slammed her hands against her hips. "I was about—"

"He put his damn hands on you, Trinity!"

"And I was about to beat his ass until you came over like a madman! I had everything under control."

"Well, it didn't look like that to me." He paced the length of the living room like a caged animal, his chest rising up and down as if he were trying to control his anger.

Trinity dropped down in one of the upholstered chairs and swiped her hands down her face. She smiled to herself at the irony of the whole situation and then a laugh erupted from the back of her throat.

Gunner stopped in the middle of the floor and looked at her with concern.

"Don't worry, I'm not crazy," she said still laughing. "It's just that I've never had a *client* come to my defense the way you did." She wiped at the tears from laughing that had slipped through her eyes.

Gunner blew out an exaggerated breath. "Listen," he drew closer and grabbed her hand, pulling her up from the chair, "I'm sorry for overreacting and if I embarrassed you, I'm sorry. I know you're more than capable of handling assholes like the guy downstairs, but the thought of him putting his hands on you..." He backed away and adjusted the baseball cap on his head. He eventually turned back to her. "I didn't like it."

Trinity only stared. "I don't know what to say. Except for 'thank you.'" She slowly approached him. "In my line of work, guys that I date just assume that I can take care of myself. So coming to my rescue or shutting down advances from other guys never happened. Your chivalry made me feel…special."

Gunner pulled her into his arms. "You are special. Very special."

He lowered his head until his lips covered hers. His tongue dueled with hers and Trinity knew she should push him away, but she couldn't. She wanted him so badly. The more time she spent with him, the weaker her defenses became. Desire and need swam through her as the battle in her head continued. It wasn't until Gunner gripped her butt that common sense kicked in.

"We should stop," she said and tried to push him away, but he tightened his grip.

"I don't think so. That kiss and the one from earlier clearly show that we are attracted to each other."

Trinity met his gaze and took a nervous swallow. Saying that she was attracted to him was an understatement. Lately he was all she thought about, whether she was awake or dreaming.

"You're right. I am attracted to you, but we can't do this. Whatever this is."

With his arms still wrapped around her, he placed feathery kisses on her cheek and worked his way down her neck.

"I disagree," he said, his voice muffled against her neck. Trinity's eyes drifted shut as she leaned into him, totally wrapped up in how good his mouth felt against her heated skin. "I think we should explore whatever this is between us and see where it goes."

Trinity opened her eyes and sighed. She had to stop this and she had to stop it now.

"Gunner." She pushed against his shoulder, this time freeing herself from his grip. "I can't do this. You're my client and I'm so sorry if I've led you on. I honestly didn't mean to. I...I...I'm sorry, we just can't do this."

Gunner leaned against the back of the chair. His gaze trained on her. "So what you're saying..." he rubbed his chin "...is that we can't see where this will lead because I'm your client."

She nodded. "Yeah. I have already behaved unprofessionally, and for that, I'm sorry. The kisses, neither of them should have happened."

"Well." He stood and moved over to the small minibar, pulling a bottled water from the refrigerator. "I'm sorry you feel that way. I guess there's only one thing to do."

Trinity tilted head. "And what's that?"

"You're fired."

Chapter 12

"What?" She rushed toward him. "What did you say?"

Gunner watched her approach, loving the fire he saw in her eyes. He knew it was wrong, but he loved rattling her. Watching her anger go from zero to ten within seconds was a serious turn-on.

"I said, you're fired. I no longer need a bodyguard." He had been thinking about this for over a week and tonight was the last straw. He wasn't fighting his feelings any longer.

"But…but, Gunner, you can't do this. We have a contract!" She jabbed him in the chest with her finger. "You can't do this to me. I need this assignment."

Gunner grabbed her finger, afraid her strong jabs would poke a hole through his chest. Seeing her anger quickly turn to distress, he knew he had to put an end to this. He held on to her hand. He snaked his free arm around her waist, pulling her close.

"Relax," he said, but she continued struggling to get free. "Trinity."

"Gunner, you don't understand," she mumbled, some of the fight going out of her. "I can't afford to lose this contract. I can't believe I allowed this to happen." She hit against his chest and he gently held her wrists.

"Sweetheart, come on now, listen to me." Gunner continued to wrestle with her, despite her trying to pull away. "I'm going to honor the contract—one hundred percent."

"I just can't afford—" she started, but stopped as if just realizing what he had said. "You're going to—"

"I'm going to honor the financial part of the contract." He held her face between his hands and kissed her lips. "I don't need a bodyguard, but I want you."

Her anxiety was shattered with the hunger of his mouth over hers, his lips soft and coaxing. Unadulterated lust engulfed Trinity as her body yearned for his touch.

"I want you." He nipped at her bottom lip and backed her toward the bedroom that he was using. Everything within Trinity turned to mush when he spoke those words—*I want you*. His voice, gentle and soothing, washed over her like a silk scarf, teasing the most sensual parts of her scorching body. "I want you... now." He lifted her into his strong arms and carried her the rest of the way.

The bedroom, with only a bedside lamp illuminating the luxury space, was as large as Trinity's condo. The majestic gold walls and draperies that accented the huge wall-to-wall mahogany headboard and platform bed made the room appear as if it were designed for royalty. Trinity soaked it all in. The five-star suites that they lived in while traveling were only a few reminders of this man's impressive wealth.

Gunner slowly set her on her feet near the satin-covered bed and her gaze met his. All the animosity she had toward him had long since vanished, and was replaced with a burning desire to have his body joined with hers. Trinity couldn't ever remember wanting a man as much as she wanted the man standing before her.

When it seemed as if he were going to just stand there, as if waiting for permission to go further, she slipped her hand under his shirt. She started at his taut abs, and then stroked his wide chest, loving the way his muscles tightened beneath her fingers. A groan rumbled within him when she worked her way up to his flat nipples, urging her on. Tweaking. Twirling. Teasing. She lifted his T-shirt over his head and her mouth replaced her fingers. Licking. Sucking. Tugging.

"Aw, baby," he ground out, his voice raspy with need. He snaked his long arm around her waist and took control. He recaptured her lips, more demanding this time. All the fight that Trinity had used over the past couple of weeks to keep a distance between them fled. Right now, she wanted nothing more than to feel every inch of this man's body against hers.

She moaned against his mouth, loving the way he had awakened the sexual need that had been brewing within her for weeks. She hadn't been with a man in over six months and Trinity had a feeling that this experience with Gunner would be like no other.

"You have on way too many clothes." He lifted her shirt over her head and tossed it to the floor. One of his hands rested on her hip, while the other gently traced a heated path between her breasts, over her ribs, only stopping when he reached her stomach. The mere touch of his fingers against her skin sent a tantalizing shiver through her body. Trinity was all for foreplay, but the fiery passion roaring through her veins was ready to be released.

"Gunner," she breathed when his hand went farther south and boldly rubbed against the V between her thighs. Trinity pushed into his touch. Even through her slacks, she could feel the heat from his hand.

He unfastened her pants and they slithered down her legs and puddled around her ankles. She stepped out of them, now clad in only her white lace bra and matching bikini panties. Gunner's intense gaze took her in from her kiss-swollen lips down to her strappy high-heeled sandals.

"You…you're absolutely breathtaking."

When he undid his belt buckle and unfastened his jeans, Trinity bent to unhook her sandals.

"Leave them," he said as he stepped out of his jeans, kicking them to the side.

Trinity had seen him in only his underwear before, but it still didn't lessen the glorious sight of him now. He stood before her in a pair of navy blue Calvin Klein briefs, the bulge of his arousal straining against them heightening Trinity's anticipation.

"I have wanted to get you naked for as long as I can remember," he said, sliding the back of his hand down the side of one of her breasts. Trinity sucked in a breath when he lowered his head to a nipple that was straining

to be free of the restrictive material. He reached behind
her and undid her bra like a professional with a flick of
his wrist. He pulled the straps down her arms and let
the material fall to the floor. "My God, girl, these are
too amazing to be hidden behind clothing.

He kissed each of the sensitive peaks.

Trinity shivered.

"Are you cold?" he mumbled, his face buried between her breasts as he massaged them between his
large hands, squeezing, caressing.

Not hardly. As a matter of fact, she was on fire.

His lips continued to explore, going lower down
her body. A small sound chirped from the back of her
throat and Gunner looked up at her. Trinity wanted to
scream for him to quit playing around and take her,
but Gunner would not be rushed. He didn't let anyone
rush him when playing poker, and Trinity knew by
instinct he definitely wouldn't let anyone rush him in
the bedroom.

He placed a lingering kiss against her damp panties
and her knees went weak. The only thing that kept her
from melting to the floor was his strong hands gripping her butt cheeks.

He glanced at her again, that sexy grin that she was
growing to love firmly planted on his tempting lips.

"You're definitely ready for me."

He lifted her effortlessly and she squeaked in surprise. Her legs went automatically around his waist as
he moved closer to the bed. He yanked the covers back
and placed her on the cold sheets, which did nothing
to tame the fire burning within her.

She scooted farther onto the bed and Gunner
grabbed her legs, halting her in place. Without a word,

his hands moved to her hips and he looped his fingers around the string of her bikinis, and slowly eased them down her legs. He brought the small strip of material to his nose and inhaled deeply. Trinity's pulse pounded, a surge of adrenaline shooting to the center of her core.

"Don't move," Gunner all but growled, the sensuous rumble of his words holding her in place. "I want to look at you." He eased his briefs down, his erection springing to life, as if happy to be free.

All Trinity could do was stare. Modesty was forgotten as she leaned back on the bed. Her elbows supported her upper body and her legs remained opened. She looked on, admiring all that made Gunner one hell of a man.

Noticing her watching, he made a production out of rolling a condom onto his thick shaft. Trinity squeezed her thighs together and bit her bottom lip, trying to hold it together. She had never been so turned on by a man as she was right then.

He climbed onto the bed and eased between her legs, his powerful erection knocking against her inner thighs.

"I'm going to do things to you tonight," Gunner started in a husky whisper, "that will have you screaming my name for years to come."

Trinity swallowed hard and her pulse increased as he moved in closer, forcing her to lie back. Desire and need swam inside her as he lowered his head and kissed her, his tongue sparring with hers, his body anchoring her to the bed. Never had she ever felt so desired by a man.

His hand eased between their bodies and found their way down to her moist heat. Trinity bucked against his fingers that slid in and out of her, stroking and teasing, nearly taking her over that cliff that she was barely hanging on to.

"Gunner," she whimpered, needing more, wanting more of him.

She reached for him. With one hand, he took both her hands and stretched them above her head, holding her in place as he continued his sweet torture.

"I know, sweetie. I can tell you're ready for me." Without missing a beat, he slid his rigid length inside her, filling her like no other.

She cried out in pleasure as her body adjusted to his size, loving every teasing stroke of his length. He inched deeper and deeper and her breaths came in short spurts. Trinity knew her release was near and tried hanging on, but she couldn't resist lifting her hips. She matched his moves stroke for stroke as his pace increased, her opening pulsating around his thickness.

"Trinity," Gunner ground out and released her hands.

He grabbed hold of her hips, his powerful thrusts growing more turbulent. He plunged in and out of her, going harder and deeper with every move. Trinity's body tightened around him, devouring the feel of him knocking against her inner walls, pushing her to the edge of her control.

"Gunner!" she screamed, when the flames of her passion roared through her body, singeing each and every nerve ending within her. "Ohmygod, ohmygod." Her thoughts fragmented as she gripped his arms, trying to hold on, her body jerking feverishly.

Seconds later, Gunner growled her name, his fingers digging into the flesh of her thighs as he pounded into her harder and faster. He surrendered to his release, shaking violently against her.

Awake for the past hour, Gunner stared down at Trinity's sleeping form, his fingers sifting through her long, thick hair. He couldn't stop looking at her. Their union had been one that he had imagined more times than not, but the reality superseded anything he could have envisioned.

She lay on her side, her knees to her chest and her hands under her cheek. Gunner lifted the bedsheet over her, reluctant to cover her shapely body. He was hard and yearning for more of what she'd given him hours ago.

He sat back against the fabric-covered headboard. By bedding Trinity, he had officially crossed a line that he couldn't uncross. He'd not only had sex with the woman who had been the star of many of his dreams, but he had also just slept with his best friend's little sister. Gunner wasn't sure if there were any rules regarding the subject, but he knew if the situation were reversed, he wouldn't think too kindly of Max hooking up with one of his sisters.

This is different, he thought. He and Max might have been the best of friends, brothers even, considering they had been in the same fraternity, but Trinity was so much more to him than his best friend's little sister. What he felt for her went so much deeper than anything he had ever experienced with any other woman. He just wasn't ready to put a title to what he was feeling.

Still playing with Trinity's hair, he glanced down to find her staring up at him.

"Good morning, sleepyhead." He scooted back

down under the covers and faced her. "Did you sleep well?"

"Very well," she said, covering her mouth when she spoke. He almost laughed. Surely she wasn't self-conscious about morning breath after all that they had shared the night before. "What time is it?"

Gunner glanced at the digital clock on his side of the bed. "Almost eleven o'clock."

She jumped up and the sheet fell to her waist. She gasped and hurried to cover her bare breasts.

He laughed. "Girl, you act as if I haven't seen everything you have. And I must say, I like everything I've seen." He went for the sheet and she slapped his hand away, making him laugh harder.

"Why didn't you wake me? We're going to miss our flight."

He shook his head. "I got us a later flight. So there's no hurry."

"Oh."

"I'm thinking that we should do a replay of last night." He kissed her lips, wrapping his arm around her waist. "What do you think?"

"I think we need to talk."

Trinity tucked the bedsheet securely around her, trying to find the right words to tell Gunner that they had made a mistake. She still couldn't believe that she had slept with him. She couldn't believe that she had slept with a client. Bile rose to her throat and her stomach tightened. Sleeping with a client went against everything she stood for. Yet having sex with Gunner was by far the most amazing experience she had ever had with a man.

Gunner propped his elbow onto his pillow and rested his head on his hand, staring up at her.

"I see the wheels turning in that pretty little head of yours," he said as if reading her mind. "Let's go ahead and talk this out, so that we can move on and not have this conversation again."

"Gunner, there is no moving on. I have committed the ultimate sin." Well, let her mother tell it, she had just committed a few sins. "I just…I just can't believe I slept with a—"

"Don't say 'client,' because technically I'm no longer your client. I fired you, remember?" He tugged on the sheet, but she held on tight. "So quit beating yourself up. I know that we started out with a business arrangement, but sweetheart, things have changed. I want so much more than a professional relationship with you. Actually, I take that back. I don't want a professional relationship between you and me. What I'm feeling right now has gone way beyond business."

"But you already paid me."

"Why don't we look at the money that I paid you as an investment? If given the opportunity, I would have been glad to invest in your company when you first opened it."

Is he for real?

"You would have done that?" she said, her voice barely a whisper.

"Sweetheart, I would do anything for you." He scooted up in the bed and moved closer to her. "There is one thing, though."

Oh, here we go. She started to move away from him but he stopped her, wrapping his arm around her shoulder.

"I know you have a business to run, but I'm wondering if you would consider staying through the end of the PPO tournament. I know you don't have to since I fired you. And I know the contract is null and void, but I'm hoping you'll want to stay. I want us to explore whatever this is that's developing between us. What do you say? Stay the next three weeks with me."

Giddiness bubbled inside Trinity. She wanted to stay, and not just because Connie would never let her hear the end of it if she returned home early. Despite her best efforts, she had to admit that she'd fallen for Gunner.

"So what do you say?" He wrapped a long arm around her waist and slid her across the bed toward him. "Will you stay?"

"Under one condition."

He cursed under his breath and dropped his head against the headboard. "You have to be the most stubborn woman I've ever met." He lifted his head and returned his attention to her. "Okay, let's hear it. What do I have to do? Learn how to cook? Teach you more poker? What?"

She let the sheet fall from her body and rose onto her knees. Gunner's dark eyebrows arched mischievously and that sexy grin that she had grown to love spread across his lips.

"Well...what do I have to do?" he croaked when she straddled him.

"Well." Her hands glided down his hard chest, her lips following behind them. Kissing. Licking. Sucking. "You have to let me continue guarding this body."

Chapter 13

"I can't believe it has taken this long for a witness to come forward," Gunner said, finishing his omelet that Trinity had prepared. A week after they had returned from New Orleans, Trinity had invited Maxwell over for breakfast. He called to let them know that the Las Vegas Police Department had caught a break with the poker player incidents.

"Was she able to give a description?"

Maxwell drank from his glass of juice. "Yeah, according to her, he's a dark-skinned black guy, tall, with short hair."

"That's it?" Gunner asked, disappointed that there wasn't more to go on. "That could be anyone."

"I know. She went through loads of photos in our database, but didn't identify anyone yet. She agreed to look through more later today."

"So basically, you guys are back to square one," Trinity said and squeezed Gunner's hand.

"Basically, but she did say he walked with a limp and that she thought he was a poker player. She'd seen him at a couple of tournaments." Maxwell leaned back in the dining room chair, rubbing his stomach.

"So what about the videotapes?" Trinity asked. "Did you guys notice anyone suspicious going in and out of the bathroom around the time of the attack?"

Maxwell shook his head. "The tapes were too fuzzy. We could see a figure leave the bathroom in a hurry around the time of the attack, but there's no way we can do a definite ID. Our tech guys are trying to clean the tape up some. I have no doubt that we're going to get this person."

"Yeah, but will it be too late?" Gunner mumbled. There were three more weeks before the championship. Though he hadn't been involved in any other incidents, he couldn't help but wonder if someone would try to get at him again.

"Trinity, girl, you still got it. I haven't had a good, home-cooked meal since I visited Momma in LA." His appreciative gaze wandered around the room. "Gunner, I still can't believe you actually have furniture in this place. It's about damn time."

"What?" Gunner looked at him, not believing what his friend was saying. "Man, you've been living in your house longer than I have and you don't have furniture."

"I have furniture in the rooms that count." He smirked.

"You both should be ashamed of yourselves." Trinity stood and started clearing the table. "It doesn't make any sense that two grown men with big houses and money don't have furniture."

"So did you pick out everything?" Maxwell asked Gunner, ignoring his sister's rant.

Gunner shook his head. "Nah, man, this is all your sister's doing." He glanced around the room, taking in the new chandelier, dining room table and wall art. Thanks to her, his first floor was fully furnished. He had to admit that he liked the house before, but with Trinity's touches, it actually felt like a home.

"So, can I get you gentlemen anything else?" Trinity asked, collecting the rest of the dishes.

Gunner watched her move around the room. She had been in his home for over six weeks and he didn't even want to think about his life going back to the way it was before she had arrived. Spending every day with her was how he envisioned spending the rest of his life.

"Gunner?" Trinity stood with her hand on his shoulder, looking at him expectantly. "Anything else?"

"Ah, nah, sweetheart, this is good." He took in her attire. Dressed the way she was in a skintight T-shirt and yoga pants with no socks or shoes, she was a temptation he could barely pass up.

Gunner's gaze followed her across the room until she left. If Maxwell wasn't there, he'd be following behind her, convincing her to forgo yoga and spend the day with him trying out some new moves in his bed.

"So what's going on between you two? What happened to the arguing or ignoring each other? You know...the usual communication style between you guys."

Gunner shrugged. "When you spend every day with

someone, you find a way to get along." And boy, were they getting along.

Maxwell poured another cup of coffee. "Question is, just how well are you guys getting along? You haven't been able to take your eyes off her since I arrived. And Trinity's not a touchy-feely type of person, yet she couldn't seem to stop touching you."

Gunner heard the edge in his friend's voice. "So what? You just been sitting there analyzing our every move? Why don't you use some of your observation skills and find the bastard who ran me down a couple of weeks ago?" Gunner's gut twisted into a knot as he tried to rein in his anger. He and Maxwell often discussed the women they were seeing, but Gunner wasn't ready to talk about Trinity.

Maxwell stared him down. If he had been a cartoon character, smoke would have been coming out of his ears. Anger radiated off him as his nostrils flared and he sat clenching his jaw, his chest heaving up and down.

Gunner fell back against his seat and sighed. "I care about your sister. A lot."

"How the hell you gon' say some crap like that to me when I know the type of player you are?"

Gunner leaned forward and gripped the table. "In all the years that you've known me, have you ever heard me admit to caring about a woman?" he said, his voice low and barely controlled. "Your sister means more to me than…than…" Gunner couldn't find the words to express what Trinity meant to him "…than anyone in my life. There is nothing I wouldn't do for her. Even fight you."

They stared each other in the eyes, seconds, then

minutes, ticking by. They were brothers and might have had their share of arguments, but they had never raised their fists at each other. But Gunner would if he had to.

Maxwell huffed. "Hurt her, and I will beat your ass."

Gunner sat back and smirked. "Yeah, like that's going to happen."

They both looked up when Trinity hurried into the room, panting. Fear gripped Gunner's body at the frantic look in her eyes and how she was wringing her hands. He leaped from his seat.

"Trinity?" His arm went around her waist when it looked as if her legs would give out. "Are you okay? What's wrong?" She was not a fragile woman, so whatever happened had to be bad.

Maxwell stood on the other side of her, gripping her elbow. "Here, sit her down."

"No. No. There's no time." Trinity wiggled out of their hold and swiped at a few tears that slipped through. "I have to go," she said in a rush. "Connie just called. Lucy was in an accident and they don't know how bad it is. I need to get to LA." She turned to Gunner. "I'm sorry, babe. I don't know if I'll make it back before tomorrow night's tournament. I'll have someone here first thing in the morning to—"

Gunner shook his head. "Not necessary. I'm going with you." He pulled out his cell phone. "Have you made flight arrangements yet?"

"No, but—"

"Good. I'll take care of it." He dialed the pilot he often used when he needed a private jet at the last minute.

"Gunner." Trinity yanked on the front of his shirt to get his attention. "I can't let you do that. I don't know how long I'll need to be there. I know how important the next couple of weeks are for you and I don't want to be the reason you miss any events."

"And I don't want you traveling by yourself when you're clearly upset." Actually, he didn't want her traveling alone, period. He knew she could take care of herself, but he had always been the protective type where women were concerned. And with Trinity, not only had his protective instincts kicked up a notch, but he also wanted to be the one to take care of her.

She released a heavy sigh. He knew she wanted to argue, but the worry for her friend was taking precedence. He could see it in her eyes and could tell by the way she paced in front of him. She was definitely worried.

"I don't know, Gunner. Maybe—"

"Trinity—" Maxwell put his arm around her shoulder, forcing her to stop moving "—you're in no condition to travel alone. Look at you. You're shaking. If I wasn't on duty later today, I'd go with you. It'll make me feel better knowing that Gunner will be by your side."

Gunner kept his gaze on Trinity while he made the arrangements. Maxwell was right. She was definitely in no condition to travel alone. He had never seen her so rattled before. She had told him all about her friends Lucy, Fred and Henry. He knew they meant the world to her.

"There'll be two of us and we need to leave as soon as possible," Gunner told the pilot on the phone. "Sure, I'll hold."

Still holding the cell to his ear, Gunner reached out and pulled Trinity close, needing to hold her for his own piece of mind. She wrapped her arms around his waist, laid her head against his chest and sighed. He placed a kiss against her temple, not believing how quickly she'd gotten into his system. There was nothing he wouldn't do for her.

A few hours later, Trinity pushed open Lucy's hospital room door, with Gunner right on her heels. Considering she was the one who was supposed to be guarding him, she appreciated the way he stepped in and took control. Prior to boarding the plane, it was as if she couldn't breathe due to worrying about Lucy. Shortly before takeoff, Connie had called to give her more details. Lucy had been hit by a car and was sporting a broken leg and a bruised hip. Trinity was thankful that her injuries weren't any worse, but at Lucy's age, those were bad enough.

Relief flooded through Trinity when she walked in and saw Lucy awake with pillows propped behind her. Trinity gave her a quick once-over. She looked even thinner than the last time she had seen her.

Lucy's eyes lit up when she noticed Trinity, but her gaze went immediately to Gunner and a small smile played around her lips. Trinity tried to fight her own smile, knowing that Lucy was going to give her the business about the handsome man by her side.

"Well, what do we have here?" Lucy said. Her voice was weaker than usual, yet her gaze didn't waiver. "I knew our girl was on assignment, but she failed to mention how handsome you are. I assume you're her client."

Gunner laughed and stepped forward. "Gunner Brooks, and I assume you're Ms. Lucy."

"Ah, so she's been talking about me. What'd she tell you?"

"Never mind what I told him. We came to check on you." Trinity moved closer to the bed. "I leave you alone for a couple of months, and you end up here. How do you feel?"

"I'm okay."

"What happened? I heard you were hit by a car."

Lucy gingerly readjusted herself on the bed. "That's pretty much it. I left Fred and Henry for a minute, needing to walk and loosen up the old bones. I stepped off a curb and—" she shrugged "—the next thing I knew I was here. A place where I can't afford to be."

Trinity knew paying for the hospital stay was foremost on Lucy's mind. "Luce, you just worry about getting better. I heard that you have a number of other health issues going on. I, for one, am glad you're here."

Lucy huffed. "Well, I won't be here long. I'm checking myself out."

"No! You're staying right here until you're all better!"

"Trinity," Gunner said, a hint of warning in his tone, his hand on her shoulder. The last thing Trinity wanted to do was upset Lucy.

"I was worried sick about you," Trinity said, her tone calmer.

"Ms. Lucy, you don't have to worry about your hospital bill," Gunner said. "Trinity's not going to relax until she knows that you're well taken care of. And I can't relax knowing that she's worried about you. The bill will be taken care of."

Trinity looked up and met his gaze. She fell in love

with him more and more every day, but when he did things like this… "Gunner—"

"Don't say anything. Just sit here and catch up with your friend. I'll take care of everything else." He kissed her lips and then left the room.

Trinity stared after Gunner. There were times when the past couple of months felt like a fantasy. A few months ago, if anyone had told her that she'd land her fattest contract ever, be attracted to a gambler and then fall in love with the man of her dreams, she would have laughed them out of the room. Gunner was turning out to be more than she could have ever imagined.

"Ahem." Lucy cleared her throat.

Trinity almost forgot Lucy was in the room and was slow to turn in her direction.

"Is there something you want to tell me?"

"Well…"

Lucy laughed and reached for Trinity's hand. "You don't have to say anything. Even with my poor eyesight, I can see the love between you two. I'm so happy for you, Trinity. If anyone deserves the happily-ever-after, it's you."

And you. Trinity wanted to say, but knew that Lucy would blow her off. "I think it's time we called your family." When she felt Lucy begin to pull away, Trinity squeezed her hand. They had talked enough about her and Gunner. It was time she talked some sense into her friend. Trinity had agreed to go back to Vegas with Gunner at least until the end of the poker finals, but she knew she couldn't leave Lucy without first knowing that she'd be taken care of. "You can't continue living on the streets, Luce. Your family loves you and wants a relationship with you. Please tell me you'll consider it. Let me call your daughter and tell her what happened."

Lucy closed her eyes. "I don't know if I can face them. I feel like such a failure."

"You are not a failure! Life has dealt you a bad hand, yet you continue to press forward. You never gave up." When Lucy gave her a *yeah, right* look, Trinity clarified. "You might be homeless, but you haven't given up on life. Despite the little that you have, you're always giving to others and you have such a beautiful spirit. It's time that you reconnect with your family so that they can experience just how wonderful you are."

They talked for a while longer and Trinity wanted to do a happy dance when Lucy agreed to let Trinity contact her family. Trinity didn't waste any time calling Lucy's daughter, who agreed to get to the hospital as soon as possible.

An hour later, Trinity stepped out of Lucy's room, glad to see Gunner.

"Perfect timing." Gunner pulled her into his embrace, placing a kiss against her expectant lips. "Why don't we go grab a late lunch before we go see your friends Fred and Henry?" Assuming Lucy was okay, they were scheduled to leave LA early the next morning in order to get back in time for Gunner's tournament.

Trinity wrapped her arms around his neck and laid her head against his shoulder. The vast array of emotions that she had experienced through the day had worn her out. She was beyond tired and longed to climb into bed and snuggle up with Gunner.

"Okay," she finally said. Trinity dropped her arms and Gunner grabbed hold of her hand, heading for the exit. They rounded a corner and Trinity stopped in her tracks, surprised to see Connie and the man standing next to her.

"What is it?" Gunner squeezed her hand and glanced around until his gaze landed on Connie.

"Hey, sis." Connie greeted her with a hug. Trinity had to admit that it was good seeing her best friend. Too bad she couldn't say the same for the man that was with her.

"Trinity."

"Ryan." Ryan Coleman, her business manager. No, make that her former business manager, who looked as though he'd rather be anywhere than there in front of her. Trinity was sure that the lethal glint he probably saw swimming in her eyes wasn't helping with his discomfort.

Trinity made introductions.

"Can we all go somewhere and talk?" Connie prompted, her gaze on Trinity. "You need to hear Ryan out before you leave town."

They followed Ryan and Connie to the corner of an empty waiting room, where they sat at a small table that had four chairs. There was no excuse for what Ryan had done to her. But by the looks of him, she could tell that he'd been through something traumatic. The dark circles beneath his light brown eyes made it look as though he hadn't slept in a while. He also appeared to have lost a considerable amount of weight. God, she hoped he wasn't on drugs. He was too handsome and too smart to go down that road.

"First, let me say that I'm sorry," Ryan started. He and Connie sat across from Trinity and Gunner. "I never meant to hurt you or put your company in jeopardy. You've been like a sister to me and the last thing I wanted to do was ruin our relationship."

"Then why did you?" Trinity tried to keep her anger at bay, but between being tired and being mad as hell at Ryan, she couldn't do it. "I could have lost everything, and all you have to say is sorry?"

"Trinity, just hear him out," Connie said.

"Well, start talking, dammit!"

Gunner placed his hand on Trinity's thigh and squeezed. She met his gaze and exhaled before returning her attention to Ryan.

Ryan stared down at his hands before lifting his gaze to meet Trinity's. "I got into some trouble with a loan shark."

"What?" Trinity couldn't believe it. Anyone who knew Ryan knew that he was the most pulled-together person there was. At one time, he had been one of the most sought-after financial advisors in LA. He had dual bachelor's degrees in finance and international business, as well as an MBA. How was it possible that he had ended up in trouble with loan sharks?

He rubbed his forehead. "I know. No one is more surprised than I am that I got myself into this mess." Taking a deep breath, he continued. "A few years ago, when I was in school to get my MBA, I ran into some financial trouble. My mother was ill. My father had just died. And I lost my financial aid due to some glitch in the system. At any rate, a friend of mine told me about this small company that loaned money—quick cash. I knew I could earn the money I needed for school, eventually, but I needed money in order to register for my classes for that following semester."

"Couldn't you get a student loan? Or couldn't the

school work with you since the financial aid glitch was on them?"

"There was no time to apply and then wait to see if the loan would come through. And it wasn't determined until months later that there had been a glitch with the financial aid." He filled her in on how the loan shark had broken into his home and showed up at his office, threatening him at gunpoint. He was told not to involve the police or he and everyone he loved would be killed. It wasn't until an undercover detective approached him for help in taking down the loan shark that the situation began to turn around.

"I left you the way I did because I didn't want anything that I did or anything that was going down to affect you or your business. In hindsight, I know I could've handled things differently—" he shrugged "—but at the time I wasn't thinking straight. These people are behind bars, your money has been returned and I have a lawyer I'm working with that will take care of any problem that might have arisen with the IRS. I just hope you can find it in your heart to forgive me."

When Trinity stood, everyone else did, too.

"Ryan—" she touched his arm "—I'm sorry you had to go through all of this. I should have known you would never do anything to intentionally jeopardize my agency. Of course I forgive you."

Chapter 14

"Are you feeling okay?" Gunner asked when he walked into the kitchen and over to the refrigerator. "You've been coughing quite a bit." He and Trinity had been back in Vegas for a couple of days and he couldn't remember her coughing before now.

"I feel all right," she said from the breakfast bar, her hands wrapped around a hot cup of something. Gunner saw the steam from across the room and could only assume she was drinking tea. It had been her beverage of choice for most of the day. "I'm a little tired and have a scratchy throat, but outside of that, I feel pretty good."

"I wonder if you're coming down with a cold." He studied her, noticing that her eyes weren't as bright as usual and her voice sounded a little hoarse. Outside of that, she did seem okay. Although, with the way his schedule had been for the past few weeks, he wouldn't be surprised if her body was fighting off something. Especially since they had been getting very little sleep. He was used to it, but he didn't think that was the case for Trinity.

"I'm fine. I rarely get sick. So I'm sure it's nothing." She set her cup down. "I know you're probably tired of poker, considering how much you've been playing lately, but I'm wondering if you'd be willing to teach me a little more about the game. Maybe we can even play a few hands."

"First of all, rarely do I get sick of poker. Secondly, I love playing with you." He saddled up behind her and wrapped his arms around her flat stomach, placing a kiss against her scented neck.

"Are we still talking about poker?" Trinity's eyes fluttered shut and she moaned softly. "Mmm, that feels good."

His lips made their way down her neck. Kissing. Nipping. Biting. His hand drew gentle circles against her abs and eased up the front of her body. He cupped her breasts, kneading them and tweaking her taut nipples. Desire rumbled through his body and blood shot to his groin. He would never get enough of caressing her soft curves or hearing her passionate moans.

Gunner growled at the ringing telephone interrupting their lust-filled moment. He didn't want to stop, but stopped anyway thinking the call was the one he was expecting from his financial advisor.

When he got up, giving one of her breasts another squeeze before moving away, the phone stopped ringing.

Figures.

"Whew." Trinity straightened her top and swiveled

around on the stool to face him. "So was that a yes to poker?"

"That's a definite yes," Gunner said, his voice heavy with longing. He wanted her right then and right there, but he had to talk to his financial advisor before the day was over. He leaned against the back of the bar stool next to Trinity, adjusting himself without being too obvious. "As a matter of fact, I think it's time that I taught you how to play strip poker."

Trinity leaned away from him and narrowed her eyes. "There you go again, trying to get me out of my clothes."

He laughed and kissed her lips. "So, is that a yes?" He placed his hands against the counter on either side of her and lowered his mouth over hers. Since their trip to New Orleans, he hadn't been able to keep his hands or his lips off her. Over the past few days, he had been a happy camper, enjoying two of his favorite things: playing poker and making love to Trinity. He had never been with a woman before who could match his hunger in the bedroom.

Trinity brought her hands up and grasped each side of his face, abruptly ending the kiss.

"Okay. Okay. I'll play strip poker with you."

"Cool." He placed another quick kiss on her lips before standing to his full height. "Meet me in the game room in an hour." He started out of the room, but stopped and turned to her. "And don't even think about putting on more layers of clothes. Can't have you cheating now, can we?"

A couple of hours later, Trinity was sorry she had agreed to play strip poker. She reached behind her back and unsnapped her bra, holding it out for him to see, and then tossed it to the floor. A shiver swept through her body and she folded her arms across her bare chest. She glanced at Gunner and rolled her eyes. He'd been wearing a mischievous grin from the time her first item of clothing had hit the floor.

"I'm starting to think that this wasn't such a good idea." She rubbed her hands up and down her arms, fighting the goose bumps popping up on her skin. Sitting in only her panties, she realized just how cold it was in the house.

"I can turn the air down if you want. Or better yet, maybe I should rub my body against yours to help keep you warm."

When he started to stand, she held up her hand. "No, you just stay over there and let's get this game over with." She was not a quitter, despite how badly she was losing.

"Suit yourself." Gunner dealt her five cards. She'd had no idea that there were different types of poker games. They were playing five-card stud and he was kicking her butt.

She glanced at her cards. She tossed two of them to the table. "Can you give me two cards, please?" Gunner dealt her two more cards. Trinity tried to prevent a smile from spreading across her mouth. Moving the cards around in her hands, she put her pair of jacks next to her pair of nines. Giddiness ran rampant through her body and she wiggled in her seat.

Gunner cocked an eyebrow at her, but didn't speak. Usually, she wouldn't have a good view of his gorgeous, dark eyes, but his lucky baseball cap was lying on the floor with her pile of clothes.

He continued to eye her, making her giddiness turn into frustration. "Would you come on and quit messing around?" she said, barely able to contain her excitement, while trying to get warm.

"What do you have?" he finally asked.

"Two pairs. Read them and weep." She stood and started doing a happy dance until he placed his cards on the table. *Three aces and two kings.* She didn't have to be a professional poker player to know that he had just beaten her again.

"Are you frickin' kidding me?" Trinity yelled. She plopped down in her seat, her breasts jiggling with every move.

Gunner grinned and slouched in his seat, his hands behind his head. "Go ahead, sweetheart, drop the panties."

Trinity narrowed her eyes. "I think you cheated. There is no way you should still have on all of your clothes and I'm only left with my underwear." She crossed her legs, her arms folded across her bare breasts.

Gunner eyed her from under lowered lids, the sexy grin still spread across his delectable lips. Trinity had no idea what he had planned when he suddenly stood. It wasn't until he lifted the tail of his shirt and slowly pulled it up past his rock-hard abs that she knew what he was doing.

"You're right. It's not fair that you be without clothes while I'm fully dressed." He lifted the T-shirt over his head, tossing it to the pile of her clothes. Trinity swallowed hard as he toed off his boots that were already untied and removed his socks. "But I must say, you look sexy as hell sitting there in just that little strip of material barely covering your fine ass."

He unbuckled his belt and the junction between her thighs throbbed in anticipation, knowing the breathtaking body that was hidden beneath his clothes. Moisture pooled in her panties. She uncrossed and then recrossed her legs, trying not to fidget under his intense gaze. With her erratic pulse pounding in her ear, she couldn't sit still.

Gunner unfastened his pants. His erection was already pushing against his jeans and it was taking everything she had to sit tight and enjoy the show. He took his time dropping his pants, his gaze steady on her. Her heart rate kicked up, beating like a conga drum inside her chest. She dropped her arms, not caring that her breasts hung freely, and swiped her sweaty palms down her bare thighs.

Her tongue slithered over her lips when Gunner grabbed hold of his bulge. Squeezing. Teasing. His black boxer briefs fitting like a second skin. When his fingers slipped inside his waistband, he inched the silk down his body, inch by excruciating inch. Trinity's knees quaked and she held on to the edge of the table when his penis sprang free and Gunner began to stroke himself. Watching her man touch himself was such a turn-on. If he kept it up, she'd have to help him and replace his hand with hers.

"Gunner..." she breathed, unable to sit still, but forcing herself not to leave her chair.

"Lose the panties, sweetheart." He stepped out of his shorts, the smoldering look in his eyes growing fiery as he dug a condom out of the pocket of his discarded jeans. His gaze remained on her as he sheathed himself.

Trinity stood, unable to pull her gaze from his amazing, hard body. She heard what he'd said, but she couldn't get her mind to will itself to obey his command. All thoughts of poker, losing and panties fled and desire filled her.

"Fine. Leave them on. I can work around them." He backed her to the wall. Bare chest to bare chest, thigh to thigh.

A whimper slipped through Trinity's lips when his mouth came down on hers, hard and possessively. Her hands had a mind of their own, as they roamed over his upper body, touching, squeezing and didn't stop until her arms flung themselves around his neck.

Gunner gripped her butt, grinding his body against hers as their tongues tangled to a familiar beat, his erection near the opening between her legs. He released her lips and kissed his way down from her cheek to her neck, nipping and licking along the way. Her heart pounded louder when his hand slipped between their bodies and then inside her panties.

"Gunner…" She squirmed against his touch, automatically opening wider for him.

"Do you know the effect you have on me," he slid a finger inside her heat, "when you're not wearing clothes?"

Trinity whimpered and her eyes slammed shut as he teased and stroked her. Her insides were turning to mush, her knees growing weak.

"Still no idea?" He slipped another finger inside her.

"Gunner!" she screamed, clawing at his shoulders and his back when his strokes became harder, more demanding.

"I'll tell you what you do to me when you don't have

on any clothes." He slid her panties down her legs and she kicked them off. His shaft replaced his fingers as he slid his length inside, stretching her until her inner muscles tightened around him. "Something within me starts as a slow, erotic churn." His strokes deepened. "Then it builds and builds until it's swirling around, bumping against other organs," he said, thrusting in and out of her harder and faster with each word he spoke. "Like a vicious tornado ready to touch down."

A scream exploded from her lips and the room spun as everything within her spiraled out of control. She squeezed her eyes shut tight, her body convulsing within his strong arms. Her nails dug into his back as he continued his sweet torture, each thrust growing more powerful than the one before.

Trinity held on for the ride, gripping his shoulders, sensing him nearing his release. His movements became more reckless. His fingers dug into the flesh of her thighs as he plunged harder and deeper, until he growled his release.

He lowered her feet to the floor and collapsed, the wall holding them both up as the aftershocks of their orgasms gripped their bodies.

"If you ever decide to give up poker," Trinity panted, her forehead against his chest, "you can always pursue a career as a stripper." She glided her hands up the back of his muscular thighs, and squeezed his butt. "With this body, you'd make a killing."

Chapter 15

The next morning, Gunner awakened to Trinity's body snuggled against him. Having her near always made him hot, but now it seemed as if he was sleeping in a hot box. He tossed the covers back and then glanced down at her naked body, surprised to see that the sheet beneath her was soaked with sweat.

What the hell?

Her hair, plastered to her forehead, hung over her face. He fingered a few strands away, but quickly snatched his hand back as if touching a hot oven. She was burning up.

Alarm bells went off in his head. The air conditioner was clearly working, so for her to be hot and sweaty, something was definitely wrong.

He leaned over her. "Trinity," he called out a couple of times, gently shaking her.

She moaned and stirred, but didn't fully awaken.

Gunner climbed out of bed and slipped into his briefs before hurrying to the bathroom for a cold, wet cloth. Grabbing an extra hand towel, he returned to his bedroom.

"Trinity?" He touched her forehead again and quickly removed his hand. His initial concern was fast turning into panic. "Sweetheart, wake up." He shook her as he patted her forehead and face with the cold towel. Normally a light sleeper, she didn't move, freaking him out even more. "Trinity!" He patted her face, intent on waking her. "Trinity!"

She moaned and tried to pull away from him. "Stop," she whined, her eyes still closed.

"Come on now, I need you to wake up." He continued to shake her.

She opened her eyes slightly, searching his face. Gunner wasn't sure if she even recognized him, seeing that she hadn't said anything yet.

"Can you sit up?" He continued to pat her forehead with the towel that was now lukewarm. "You're burning up. I need to get you to a hospital. Come on, let me help you up."

"No…my whole body aches. My throat hurts," she said so quietly, Gunner had to strain to hear. She tried to curl up, but Gunner wouldn't let her. "I'm so tired."

"I know, sweetie. You're sick. I need to get you to a doctor."

"I'm okay." She had a loose grip on his arm, a scorching heat from her touch surging through his body. Usually the heat she emitted turned him on, but this wasn't normal. Icy fear twisted around his heart.

If anything happened to her… He shook his head. This was no time to think the worst.

He debated in his mind whether to wrestle with her to get her up and dressed. She needed a doctor.

Leaping over the bed, he grabbed his cell phone and dialed.

"Hey, little bro," his sister answered on the first ring. "I'm surprised to hear from you this time of day. Is everything all right?"

"Actually, no." He paced at the foot of his bed, rubbing his forehead. "My gir…my…" His voice cracked as he tried to get the words out. *Hell, I don't even know what to call her.*

"Gunner, what's going on?" his sister asked, worry in her voice. "Are you okay?"

He cleared his throat. "No. I mean yes. I'm fine. But my girlfriend is sick and I'm not sure what to do."

Seconds passed before she spoke. Gunner knew she was surprised to hear him refer to any woman as his girlfriend. That was a first for him, and his sister knew it.

He moved back over to Trinity, and dabbed at beads of perspiration near her hairline.

"Sick how? What's—"

"Jewels, she's burning up and I don't know what do!" he yelled, surprising himself. His sister was an RN and, unlike him, was used to dealing with sick people.

"Okay, first of all, you need to calm down," she said. "Since I'm sure you don't have a thermometer, I'm going to assume that burning up means she has a fever. You're going to need to get her fever down. Has she complained about any aches or pains?"

Gunner sat on the side of the bed and stared down

at Trinity, feeling helpless. "Yeah. She says her throat hurts and her body aches."

"How was she yesterday?"

"She was fine," he said. Their game of strip poker and the wild activities that followed came to mind. "Wait. Earlier in the day, she was sneezing and complaining about having a scratchy throat."

"Hmm, she might have the flu, or at least that's what it sounds like."

"So what should I do? Should I take her to emergency?" Gunner wet the towel again and pressed it against Trinity's face and neck.

"Do you know if she's allergic to anything?"

"Tomatoes." During dinner a few weeks ago, he had offered her some of his tomato bisque and she had mentioned having an allergy toward them.

"Okay, grab a sheet of paper. I'll give you a list of things you're going to need from the store and what you can do to get that fever down." Jewels rattled off over-the-counter meds, along with things he'd need from the grocery store. The more she told him, the calmer he became, feeling more confident that he could nurse Trinity back to health.

"All right, sis. I'm going to work on this list and see what happens."

"Good. Give it a day and her fever should break. If it doesn't, get her to a doctor."

"Will do."

"So this woman must be pretty important to you if you're this worried."

Gunner glanced across the bedroom from his sitting area. "Yeah, she is," he finally said. "She's very important to me."

They talked for a few minutes longer before Gunner disconnected. Since he had no intention of leaving Trinity alone, he made some calls to get everything on the list delivered.

Gunner moved back to the bed and stood over Trinity's sleeping form. *She's very important to me.* The words rattled around in his head. His heart swelled as he realized just how much he cared for her.

He bent down and placed a kiss on her forehead, then caressed her cheek with the back of his hand. "I need you to get well so that you can go back to giving me hell."

Trinity snuggled deeper into the oversize leather chair, a blanket wrapped around her legs and a cup of tea cradled between her hands. For the past three days, she'd been stuck in the house, with Nurse Gunner Brooks tending to her every need. If someone had told her weeks ago that she'd be camped out in Vegas with a hot, sexy professional poker player, she would have laughed in their face. Never in a million years would she have imagined the relationship that had grown between them.

"I'm glad to see you relaxing," Gunner said when he walked into the theater room, balancing a huge bag of chips, juice, bottled water and a thermos, no doubt filled with soup, for her. Trinity was pretty sure that she had consumed ten gallons of soup in the past few days and couldn't take any more.

"What else would I be doing? My self-appointed nurse will barely let me go to the bathroom without fussing over me or sweeping me off my feet in order to save my energy."

Gunner set everything he'd carried into the room onto the small table near Trinity's seat. "Why do you have to call me a nurse? Why not 'doctor' or even better, why not call me 'the sexy hunk'?"

Trinity's mouth dropped open. "How…" Her voice trailed off as she saw the wicked grin planted firmly on his enticing lips. Connie had called her cell phone earlier that day. Her friend must have said something to Gunner, because no way would he come up with that on his own.

Trinity sipped from her still-too-hot tea. "I think calling you *Doctor* is pushing it a bit."

"Well—" he dropped down into the seat next to Trinity "—feel free to call me 'sexy hunk' anytime." Trinity rolled her eyes. She was going to kill Connie. "So who's winning?"

Gunner turned the volume up on the big screen that covered a complete wall in the theater room. It was the NBA playoffs and this was the first day that Trinity felt well enough to leave the bedroom. Normally not a big fan of basketball, if it meant getting out of bed for a few hours, she'd even watch *The Three Stooges* if necessary.

"What time is your tournament tomorrow?" Trinity asked. Her timing for getting sick was good in relation to his poker schedule. The PPO, the longest poker series, was scheduled to start the next day. Trinity knew that the next few weeks were going to be super busy.

"It starts at noon." He stuffed a handful of chips into his mouth and followed it up with a long swig of water. "But you're not going."

Trinity leaned away from him. "Excuse me?"

Gunner glanced at her, apparently noticing the lethalness behind her words. "What?" He set his water down. "You're not well enough to go anywhere yet and these tournaments are long and demanding. Nah…" He shook his head. "I want you to stay in a few more days."

Trinity appreciated his concern for her health, but he was taking this caregiver role a little too far. "I think I know whether or not I'm well enough to do something. I have no fever, and my energy is back. Besides, when I first took on this assignment, we agreed that you wouldn't go anywhere without me. Have you forgotten that there's still a crazy person out there taking out poker players?"

Gunner sighed loudly. "I haven't forgotten, but I don't want you going anywhere until you're one hundred percent. *Besides*, I fired you. Remember?" He returned his attention back to the game as if the conversation was over.

Trinity glared at him. She remembered, all right. That amazing night in his hotel suite would be forever embedded in her mind. But she wasn't letting him go anywhere alone. At least not until they found out for sure if there really was someone targeting PPO favorites.

Trinity set her mug down and laid her head against the high-back seat. She appreciated Gunner's concern regarding her health, and had accepted the strong feelings she had for him. But there was no way in hell she was going to stop being his bodyguard. They had an agreement. He might've been willing to pay out the contract without her doing any work, but that wasn't how she operated. She took her job seriously. Unfortunately, she had set aside her professionalism and slept with a client, but she never walked away from an agreement before it was fulfilled.

"I'm going," she said suddenly. "And as for me being fired, I've reinstated myself. I'm your bodyguard whether you like it or not. And I will be your bodyguard until you have officially secured one of the nine spots in the November event. So," she said with a cocky attitude, "you are stuck with me until the middle of July when they announce who the nine people are that will compete in November." She gathered her mug and blanket and walked out of the room, leaving him with his mouth hanging open.

Damned stubborn woman. Gunner shook his head. Of all the women he could have fallen in love with, he wondered why he had to choose the most stubborn woman on the face of the earth.

Gunner gulped down the rest of his water, but suddenly jerked forward in his seat. Coughing and sputtering at the last thought, he pounded his chest.

Love. Was he really in love with Trinity?

He had to admit she was everything he wanted in a woman: intelligent, sophisticated, independent and her being sexy as hell didn't hurt. Lately, he had been thinking more and more about getting married and having a family. He would be thirty-one on his next birthday. According to his dad, it was past time for him to settle down with one woman. Not knowing that he and Trinity would hit it off the way they had, he was now glad he had followed through in seeking her out for protection.

The only issue—determining if Trinity felt the same way.

The next day, Gunner helped Trinity out of the car when their driver pulled up in front of the Rio All-Suite

Las Vegas Hotel. They were there for the first tournament of the PPO.

He squeezed her hand. "Are you sure you're going to be okay hanging out here for the next few hours?"

"Gunner if you ask me that one more time, I'm going to scream." They weaved in and out of people as they made their way through the casino. "I've already told you, I'll be fine."

Gunner had to admit that she looked like her old self. The color was back in her cheeks. She seemed to have more energy than she'd had in the past few days. And as sexy as she looked in her outfit, he was pretty sure he would probably have to kick someone's ass before the night was over. He loved it when she wore her hair in large curls, bouncing against her shoulders. She was dressed in a one-shoulder red shirt, fitted white slacks, and white wedge-heel sandals, and he hadn't been able to take his eyes off her.

Before they reached the card room, Gunner pulled her off to the side and into a short hallway. He backed her against the wall and leaned in, only inches from her mouth.

"I'm a little hesitant to take you into this room with you looking as hot as you look. How the hell am I supposed to concentrate?"

The left corner of her ruby-red lips tilted into a wanton smile and Gunner's heart skipped a beat. He ground the lower part of his anatomy against her, unable to help himself. His instinctive response to her body was so powerful.

Trinity ran her hands up his chest. "You're a professional, Mr. Brooks. I have no doubt you'll be able to rack up thousands of chips tonight."

"You think so, huh?" He leaned in closer to her mouth, taking her bottom lip gently between his teeth, and then her top lip.

"I know so." Her voice, a hoarse whisper, was like an arrow shooting desire straight to his groin.

"I love you," he said, shocking himself, his heart beating wildly in his chest. By the look on Trinity's face, he had shocked her, as well. He held the sides of her face between his hands and kissed her. He was glad he had finally said the words aloud. "Sweetheart, I love you so damn much."

"Oh, Gunner!" She threw her arms around his neck, tears brimming in her eyes. "Baby," she said between kisses, "I love you, too. More than I could ever express."

He leaned in to her, intent on letting her feel what she'd done to him. Each day with her was like waking up to sunshine and clear blue skies. He couldn't believe how, in only a few weeks, she had swept into his life and changed it for the better.

"If we weren't in such a public place, I would take you right here and right now."

"And I might let you, but we have to get going so that you're not late." She attempted to pull away, but he held firm. "All right," she said nonchalantly and relaxed within his arms. "If you don't care about being late, we can stay out here all night."

With the slight erection pushing against his zipper, it would be a while before he could leave that spot, at least not without embarrassing himself. He trailed soft kisses along her cheek and near the back of her ear, one of her erogenous areas. He loved the way she wiggled against him whenever his lips went near her ears.

"God, you smell good," he whispered.

His mouth covered hers before she could respond. It was as if he were floating, his tongue exploring the inner recesses of her mouth. He still could not get enough of her. Her arms tightened around his neck and she pulled the back of his head forward, increasing the pressure of their kiss. Now that he had experienced what it would be like to have Trinity in his world, he had no intentions of letting her ever walk out of his life. He wanted her in every way a man could want a woman, and he planned to make her his, permanently.

I love you.

Those three words rattled around in Trinity's head. She knew the exact moment she fell in love with Gunner, the night he had roughed up the guy in New Orleans. That same night, they made love for the first time. But the thought of him loving her was more than she could wish for. She smiled to herself, thinking of how everything had played out. Had he not insisted on her being his bodyguard, she never would have known how wonderful a man he was.

She settled back in her seat and prepared for the long evening ahead.

Four hours into the tournament and Trinity was starting to think that maybe Gunner was right. Maybe it was too soon for her to be out. She felt like crap. The slight throb in her head from earlier had turned into a full-blown headache and she was afraid that if she sat back down, she'd fall asleep. Instead, she stood near a wall where she could still keep an eye on Gunner and prayed that the game would be over soon.

Trinity glanced back at his table, noticing that his

chip stack was continuing to grow and there was only him and two other people left at the table. Whenever he made eye contact, she looked away. If he knew she was fading fast, there was no telling what he would do. Earlier, he had offered to skip the event, claiming it wouldn't hurt his chances of being one of the top nine by the end of the PPO. He had apparently forgotten that he had told her that it was important that he participate in as many events as he could. In addition to cash prizes, tonight's winner would walk away with a poker bracelet. If Gunner won, it would be the sixth one in his career. Trinity didn't want to be the reason he walked away empty-handed.

"Can I get you anything?" a server with a very tiny skirt asked.

"No, thank you, I'm fine," Trinity answered. A strong black cup of coffee would have been great, but rarely did she drink or eat while on assignment. Then again, this wasn't an ordinary assignment.

Chapter 16

What in the hell is wrong with me?

Now, three weeks into the series, Gunner had already dropped out of the top five, something that rarely happened.

Gunner toyed with the cards. He couldn't believe the last three rounds. He had miscalculated and made some stupid bets. If he didn't get his act together, and quick, he could kiss his chance of winning goodbye. More important, he risked not getting a seat at the final table.

"What's up, Brooks? You tryin' to make this easy for me tonight?" Roman Jeers taunted from across the table. "Keep playing like this and I'll be a shoo-in for the finals."

Gunner glared at him, knowing that his nemesis was right. All it would take was a few more mistakes and Gunner could kiss the PPO championship goodbye.

A renewed energy surged through his veins. He had

worked too long and far too hard to just let someone snatch this round from him.

He lifted the corners of his two cards, knowing what they were, but needing to think about his next move. He didn't need to glance around the table to remind himself that some of the chip stacks were high. But he still held an edge. He had started the night with one and a half million in chips. Larry and Carl, the goofballs of the group, were barely hanging on with maybe three hundred thousand in chips. It was currently the two of them, Gunner, loudmouth Roman and the newbie remaining at their table.

"Any day now, Brooks," Roman smirked, his words laden with cockiness.

Rarely did Gunner speak while playing poker. He let his winning hands do all of his talking. He took longer than necessary in placing his bet so that he could torture his opponents. Raise their anxiety. He glanced at Roman. He knew the man did most of his yapping when he was nervous. And he'd been doing a lot of talking this round.

Gunner held Roman's gaze, not missing the way he kept swiping away the beads of sweat at his hairline. It was time Gunner raised the stakes. He pushed one hundred and twenty-five thousand in chips to the middle of the table, then sat back and watched. His grandfather had often told him to go big or go home.

"I fold," Larry said and tossed in his cards. Carl followed suit.

There was no one sitting to Gunner's right, but two seats over, the newbie twirled a few chips in his hands. Gunner had been the last to go before the dealer turned down the next card. Gunner knew that he'd taken a chance with his large bet. His gut told him that this hand would put him back at the top tonight.

The dealer dealt the fourth card.

Minutes passed before Newbie stood. "I'm all in," he said, surprising the heck out of everyone. Gunner studied him, thinking that he was bluffing, but not sure.

"Ah, damn. Why you wanna go and do a thing like that, young man?" Roman let out a loud, wicked laugh. "Now I'm going to have to call you." He put in the same amount of chips as Newbie and then smirked at Gunner. "Now what you gonna do, Brooks?"

It's time to shut you up.

Gunner pushed out another stack of chips, raising the pot more than three times the blind.

Newbie shook his head and Roman glared at Gunner.

The dealer put down the last card. *Ace of hearts.*

Newbie cursed, throwing his cards in before he left the table. Cheers went up behind them. Roman dropped down in his chair and tossed his cards in.

"You lucky son of a bi—"

Gunner tuned him out as a wave of relief swept through him. He felt as if he had just run a marathon, but all that mattered was that he had won the round. If his luck held on, he'd be the last man at the table.

He glanced over at Trinity, who had been sitting on the edge of her seat, and winked. Everything in him wanted to go over and kiss her square on the mouth, but she was the reason he practically had to do his version of a poker Hail Mary. For the past few weeks, she was all he had been able to think about. He loved her more than anything, but right now she was a distraction he couldn't afford.

* * *

"I'm glad we decided to stay here at the hotel tonight." Trinity kicked off her shoes and placed them in the closet. "I am dog tired. I don't know how you guys play night after night with such intensity."

From her vantage point, while watching Gunner play, it looked as if he had lost more hands than usual. But toward the end, he made his comeback and ended up being the last man at the table. She was so happy for him. He had won another bracelet weeks ago to add to his collection and was now inching his way to the top, having one of the largest chip counts.

Trinity removed her earrings and placed them inside their velvet pouch. Looking into the mirror, she noticed Gunner standing behind her near the bed, flipping through television channels. He hadn't said much on the way upstairs to their suite, and had said even less since arriving in their room.

"Baby, you okay?" she asked and eased up behind him, wrapping her arms around his narrow waist. He maintained his stance in front of the television, still flipping through channels. "Can I get you anything?"

Gunner covered her hand with his. "Nah, I'm good." He pulled out of her light hold and dropped down on the bed. He removed his boots and then stretched out. "I think I'm going to call it a night." His mumbled words were laden with exhaustion.

Trinity stood over him, her weight shifted to one side, her hand on her hip. She had big plans for him tonight. The sexy little see-through nightie that she'd ordered had arrived yesterday and she had planned to model it for him tonight. Normally after he finished playing, he was all over her. But now he lay there with his knees pulled up and an arm draped over his eyes.

A slight smile formed on her lips. Gunner wasn't one to turn down a night of passionate lovemaking, no matter how tired he was. She grabbed her overnight bag and carried it into the bathroom. Once he saw her in her new lingerie, sleep would be the last thing on his mind.

Fifteen minutes later, Trinity stood in front of the bathroom mirror, showered and feeling sexier than a Victoria's Secret model looked. She loved the way the soft material hugged her curves and stopped just below her butt. Giddiness rattled inside her when she imagined Gunner's reaction. If she turned him on when fully dressed, she had no doubt that her skimpy outfit would have him energized and ready to make love in no time.

Trinity took one last look in the mirror and strutted into the bedroom. The soft light sneaking through the partially opened bedroom door revealed that Gunner was in the living room. *Hmm, I thought he was tired.*

"Gunner?" she called out before walking into the living room of the two-bedroom suite. She found him standing in front of the refrigerator, with the door wide open and him staring inside. She cleared her throat. When he glanced up, she strolled across the width of the living room, making a few twists and turns, ensuring that he got a good look at what he was getting tonight.

She stopped and struck a pose.

Gunner's gaze raked slowly down her body. For the first time, Trinity couldn't tell if he liked what he saw or not. Normally there would be a slow smile or a sexy grin lighting up his features. But right now, his expression was blank.

"You don't like it?" she asked, hating how whiny her voice sounded. "I thought maybe..."

He stayed where he was, across the room. Her heart sank. She folded her arms over her chest, wishing she could crawl into a cave and never come out. What had she been thinking? Clearly he preferred to be the aggressor, and here she was trying to seduce him.

She turned to head back into the bathroom.

"Wait." Gunner crossed the room to her. He placed his hand on her arm, but pulled it back just as quickly. "Sweetheart, I love the outfit. Thank you for modeling it for me."

Anger soared through her veins quicker than she could rein it in. "I wasn't planning to just model it for you. I thought you'd be interested in seeing what was underneath it, but apparently not."

"Come on, Trinity." He turned away, snatching his baseball cap off his head and tossing it to a nearby chair. "I told you I was tired and just wanted to get some rest. It's been a long day. Hell, it's been three long days. Until tonight, I wasn't even sure I was going to still have a chance at the final table this year."

"But, Gunner, you're back on top. What's the big deal? You still have a couple of weeks—"

"What do you mean, what's the big deal? The big deal is that this is my *job*, my livelihood. Anything can happen in the next couple of weeks." He paced in front of her but stopped. "You've witnessed it yourself. A player can be leading one day and in fifth place the next. I can't afford to take that chance." He rubbed his forehead. "All I'm asking is for you to understand. I just need to relax so that I can get back on track."

"Fine! Get some rest." She stormed into the bathroom, slamming the door behind her.

Gunner cursed under his breath. Not only was he feeling like crap because of the way he played tonight, but now Trinity was mad at him. He could've handled things better. The last thing he wanted was to hurt her.

He went back to the refrigerator and popped open a can of apple juice, taking a long gulp. A vision of Trinity in her skimpy outfit floated around in his head. He wanted her more than he wanted to breathe, but he wasn't strong enough. He lacked self-control when it came to Trinity. If he had touched her... He shook his head and sipped his juice. In order to get his head back into the game, he had to keep his hands off Trinity. She was sexy in regular clothes, but having her scantily clad in see-through lingerie was definitely his kryptonite.

Gunner took his juice into the living room and plopped down on the sofa. He couldn't seem to get tonight's game out of his head. He had played like crap, definitely not like a man who wanted to win the championship.

He glanced toward the bedroom when he heard Trinity bumping around. Part of him wanted to go and check on her, but the other part of him knew it was a bad idea.

Instead of camping out on the sofa, he decided to go to bed. Rarely did he doubt his poker-playing abilities, but his stomach was in knots trying to figure out how to balance his love for poker and his love for Trinity. Right now, he was on track to win the PPO championship. It would be one of the biggest accomplishments of his career. And that's where his focus needed to be.

Turning off the television and all but one light, he grabbed his drink and stood at the door to their bedroom, and debated on entering. *I'm not in the mood for an argument.* He turned and went into the suite's other bedroom.

The next day, Gunner pulled into the garage and pushed the button to let the overhead garage door back down. Trinity couldn't believe that they had spent the twenty-minute ride back to his house in almost complete silence.

He removed their weekend bags from the trunk of the car and went into the house, not bothering to wait for her. But what had she expected? When he ignored her seduction efforts the night before, she thought that maybe he needed the night to regroup. He seemed really upset about the way he'd been playing. Yet this morning, she awakened to his same sullen attitude. He hadn't even joined her in the shower, which was something he had done most days over the past few weeks. She thought that after grabbing lunch and then heading home, he would be in a better mood.

They needed to talk. She had had about all that she could take from his funky attitude.

She stormed into the house, slamming the door behind her. When she didn't find him in the kitchen, she marched up the stairs.

"What is your problem?" she demanded when he walked out of her bedroom, now with only his bag. Considering they'd been sharing his bedroom, this made her even angrier. Apparently, he was letting her know without saying the words that they were no longer sharing a bed. "You acted like a jerk last night. I put up with it, trying to give you some space, but I've had enough." She followed him into his bedroom. "Did something happen while we were at the tournament? Did I do something? Did I say something that offended you? What the heck is going on?"

He dropped the bag abruptly and spun on her, catching her off guard. Instinct had her stepping back and getting into a fighting stance. Gunner looked at her as if she had lost her mind.

"You honestly think I would strike you?" His voice held a tinge of shock and disappointment. "I would never, *ever*, put my hands on you to hurt you."

She shook her head and dropped her arms. "I know. I know. That was a reflexive move." She stepped toward him, her hands on his chest. "I need to know what's going on."

"Sweetheart." He cupped her cheek with his hand, and then quickly dropped his arm. "There is nothing going on. Except my chip count fell way down this weekend and that's something I can't afford."

When Trinity approached him, he turned and grabbed his bag, placing it on the bed. Maybe she was being overly sensitive, but it seemed as if he was pulling away from her.

She watched as he unpacked his bag, placing some things in drawers and others in the dirty clothes hamper.

"Is there anything I can do to help?" She leaned against one of the bedposts at the foot of the bed, running her hand over the smooth cherry wood. "I know I'm not great at poker, but maybe there's something I

can do to help you practice." She immediately thought
of their game of strip poker and an idea popped into
her head.

She approached him with a lustful smile, hoping to
lighten the mood. Wrapping her arms around his waist,
she rested her head against his strong back.

"Why don't we play a game of strip poker? Then
maybe we can relax a little in that swimming pool that
you call a bathtub."

He patted her hand and pulled away from her. "Not
today. Right now, I just want to get settled and regroup.
Maybe another day," he said over his shoulder en route
to the master bathroom. "I'll see you tomorrow." He
closed the door, leaving Trinity staring after him.

Tomorrow? Was he honestly planning to spend the
rest of the afternoon and night holed up in his bedroom?

Fifteen minutes later, Gunner sat in his sauna, his
eyes closed, and his head resting against the wood-
paneled wall, sweat pouring down his body. He knew
he had disappointed Trinity, but he couldn't help it. He
kept replaying his last poker game over in his mind. By
the end of the night, he had gotten his chip count up,
putting him in third place overall, but it wasn't good
enough. He wanted to be in first place going into the
next couple of weeks of the tournament. He should have
been in first place. He could blame some of it on the
cards not going his way, but he knew the real problem.

The last month and a half of traveling around the
country and living with Trinity had been wonderful.
Unfortunately, spending so much time with her had

taken him off his game, especially once they became intimate.

Gunner stepped out of his sauna and grabbed a towel. Standing in front of the mirror, he wiped the sweat from his face and stared at his reflection. He looked tired. Hell, he was tired and frustrated. Besides that, the woman he loved was probably feeling neglected, and he wasn't quite sure what to do about it.

He stepped into his walk-in shower, hoping that the cold water would wash away some of the uncertainty floating around in his mind.

Chapter 17

Days later, Trinity sat at the kitchen table, picking over her dinner. She hated eating alone. The smothered fried chicken and rice was good, but not having anyone to share it with was downright depressing.

Gunner, holed up in his game room for the past two hours, hadn't shared a meal with her in days. She had even set a time for dinner, thinking that just maybe it would make a difference in whether he came out of his room or not. Apparently, spending time with her wasn't as important. Why she expected this day to be any different from the past few days was a mystery.

Covering her face with her hands, she wanted to scream. *How could I have been so stupid? What was I thinking?* She had done everything she vowed not to do. She slept with a client, foregoing professionalism. She fell for a gambler and, worst of all, she fell in love with Gunner.

Her heart tightened inside her chest as sadness fell upon her. She had never felt so lonely in all her life. After breaking so many of her rules during this assignment, she had hoped it would lead to a happily-ever-after.

Unable to eat any more, Trinity took her plate to the sink. Lately, each conversation she started with Gunner fell flat after only a few words from him. Now she was tired of trying. Tired of trying to get him to talk to her. His disinterest was too much like what her mother went through with Trinity's father, with the nights alone, her father's sullen moods, and poker dominating all of his attention. The only difference was that Trinity wasn't scrambling around in search of money to pay the mortgage or looking for lunch money for her kids.

She finished putting away the food and cleaning the kitchen. With only a week and a half to go of tournaments, she was more than ready to return to her life in LA.

"Sorry I missed dinner." Gunner walked into the kitchen and kissed her on the cheek. Trinity's heart leaped from his nearness, but gone were the days when he would wrap his arms around her and grind his hard body against her derriere. "Time kind of got away from me." He grabbed a soda from the refrigerator, opened it and then sifted through the mail that sat on the breakfast bar.

Sadness enveloped her in a tight hold. *What happened to "I love you and I can't imagine living the rest of my life without you"?*

She kept her back to him as she wiped down the counter, hoping to hide the hurt that she was feeling on the inside. Within a week, things had changed between them and she didn't know if she could handle much more of his blasé attitude.

She grabbed her glass of white wine from the table and headed out of the kitchen. "Your plate is in the microwave." Trinity walked past the breakfast bar and accidently knocked her handbag from one of the bar stools. *That's just great.* She set her glass down and stuffed everything back into her bag, but stopped when she spotted the green emerald next to the leg of the bar stool.

Picking it up, Trinity sat back on her haunches and held the gorgeous stone up to the light. She twirled it between her fingers as a niggling feeling settled in her gut. *Where have I seen this before?*

"Trinity?"

She heard Gunner's voice, but ignored him. She had a feeling that there was something important about the gem. She just couldn't figure out what it was. Then out of nowhere, a burst of recognition settled in her mind. "Oh, my God," she said just above a whisper. "I think I know who's behind the attacks."

"What? Who?" Gunner grabbed hold of her elbow to help her stand, but she shook him off, not ready to let go of the disappointment she felt toward him. She knew it was childish, but she couldn't help it. He had practically ignored her for the past few days and the sooner they caught whoever was behind the attacks, the better. It was time for her to go home, and time for her to get Gunner out of her system.

Gunner shoved his hands into the front pockets of his jeans, but removed them when she handed him the emerald.

Watching as he held it up, turning it back and forth,

Trinity hated that things couldn't have turned out differently between them. Her heartbreak was her own fault, though. She shouldn't have ever gone against her better judgment, first getting involved with a client and worse, a gambler. She shook herself, getting back to the matter at hand.

"What's the guy's name who toys with a brass-looking key ring while playing poker?" When Gunner looked confused, she said, "You know, the guy who you *slammed* against the wall a few weeks ago. What's his name? I haven't seen him at the last couple of tournaments."

"Who? Simon…Simon McCallum?" Gunner returned the jewel to her outstretched hand.

"Yeah, that's him."

"Hold up, wait. What does the emerald have to do with anything and why do you think Simon's behind the attacks?"

Trinity pulled out her cell phone and dialed her brother's number before returning her attention back to Gunner. Staring into his gorgeous brown eyes still made her weak in the knees. Of all the people she could've fallen in love with, why'd it have to be him?

"I found this near the bathroom where Jeff was attacked. I forgot all about it until now, but I'm almost positive that it belongs to him. If I remember right, the last time I saw him toying with the key chain it was missing a stone. He might not be behind the attacks, but he fits the witness's description and he walks with a limp. As of right now, he's a person of interest." Trinity turned away from Gunner when Maxwell answered his phone. "Max, I might've stumbled upon something regarding the case. Can you check out Simon McCallum?"

* * *

Gunner watched as Trinity headed toward the stairs, talking on her cell phone. The possibility of Simon being behind the attacks was crazy. He might be a jerk sometimes, but he had just as good of a chance as anyone to win the PPO. Why would he risk it? Gunner shook his head. *It can't be Simon. It doesn't make sense.*

Gunner opened the microwave. Spotting the plate of food, he closed the door and heated his meal. He had mixed feelings about the case possibly being solved. On the one hand, he wanted whomever was responsible, whether it was Simon or someone else, caught. On the other hand, once this person was caught, Trinity's duties would officially be over. He didn't miss the way she had pulled away from him when he tried to help her stand. He played the past few days around in his mind and he could see why she would be mad at him. So engrossed in getting his head back in the game, he had all but ignored her.

The microwave timer chimed and he pulled the hot plate out and took it back over to the breakfast bar. He inhaled, closing his eyes as the amazing aroma wafted from the meal. If Trinity was anyone else, he would be leery about eating any parts of the dinner, afraid that she'd done something to it, like spit in it. But she wasn't the vengeful type. If she were, he probably would've known it already.

He cut into the chicken and stuck a piece into his mouth, savoring how the meat practically melted in his mouth. *Man, this girl can cook.* One of many things he loved about her. Eating his meal, all he could think about was how much of an idiot he'd been. Part of him knew he needed to make things right with Trinity, but the other part of him thought she should understand why he needed a little space. He had never been a good communicator, and this was one of many things he needed to work on if he were going to make things right with the woman he loved.

Gunner finished off the meal and stood to take the plate to the sink. The moment he reached for the faucet, he heard Trinity on the stairs. Setting the plate down, he walked out of the kitchen, but stopped short.

"Hey, hey, what's going on?" He blocked her path, not missing the tears in her eyes and the luggage in her hands. "Where are you going?"

"I have to go." She tried moving around him, but he wouldn't let her. He removed the suitcases from her hands and set them down.

He held on to her arm to keep her from grabbing the luggage. "Talk to me. If this is about my behavior—"

She shrugged out of his grip. "It's too late, Gunner. I'm going home."

"Sweetheart, I can't let you leave. Especially like this. We need to talk." Gunner had never been so afraid of losing anyone in all of his life. He couldn't let her walk out of that door. He couldn't let her walk out of his life.

Trinity shook her head and stepped out of his reach. "Please. I have to... I can't do this...us, anymore." She took a deep breath, clearly trying to get her emotions under control. "It was a mistake. What we did...what *I* did. I can get you another guard or—"

"No!" Gunner yelled, not meaning to raise his voice, but glad he had her attention. "We've already been through this. I don't want anyone else." He approached her, but stopped when she took a step back. He ran his hand over his head. If he let her leave, there was no telling if he would ever see her again. "Sweetheart, I know…"

He started, but stopped when a horn honked outside.

"I called a cab to take me to the airport." She moved to the door. When she grabbed the doorknob, he placed his hand over hers.

"I'll take you to the airport. All I'm asking is that you hear me out." When she didn't say anything, he took that as a good sign. It was also a good sign that, when he glanced through the small window in the door, he noticed the cab pulling away from the curb. "Let me grab a couple of things from upstairs."

When she didn't argue, he dashed upstairs. He had to talk her into staying. He tossed a couple of things into his duffel bag just in case she followed through on getting on an airplane. If she did, he would be right behind her. He grabbed his lucky hat, and practically jumped down the stairs.

"Trinity?" He glanced around until he heard the overhead garage door. "Oh, damn."

He dashed through the kitchen and out the door just as she started up the car. Not bothering to say anything, he jumped into the passenger seat. *Would she have really left without telling me?*

They rode in silence for the first five minutes of the ride. Gunner knew he hadn't been the easiest person to live with over the past couple of weeks, but he couldn't help it. He didn't do serious relationships…until now. And trying to find that happy medium between Trinity and poker was proving to be harder than he would have ever thought. He couldn't figure out how to balance the two.

"Listen," Gunner started. Apologizing didn't come easy for him, but he had to try. "I'm sorry."

Trinity glanced at him and then returned her attention back to the street. "For what? For making me miss my ride to the airport or for being a jerk?" She divided her attention between him and the road. "Or are you sorry for telling me that you love me when you clearly didn't mean it?"

Gunner rubbed the back of his neck and stared out the passenger-side window. He should have known that she wasn't going to make this easy.

"When I told you that I loved you, I meant it."

"Well, dammit, Gunner. Why have you been treating me like you don't want me around?" She wasn't crying, but Gunner heard the anguish in her words. "You didn't make me feel loved. One minute I'm feeling like the most important person in your world and lately you've made me feel like...like you don't want me. Like I'm an intrusion."

Gunner held on to the door handle when she made a right turn on two wheels. A wave of apprehension swept through him when she shifted gears and her speed increased from forty-five to eighty within seconds. The dealer who sold him the BMW Alpina B7 said it could go from zero to sixty in 4.2 seconds, but Gunner had no intentions of ever testing it out.

They sped down the street, the landscape out the window a blur. There weren't many people on the road, but Gunner didn't want to end up in an accident. Starting this conversation while she was behind the wheel of his car might not have been one of his better decisions.

"Sweetheart, slow down before you kill us both."

"I can't," she said, her tone a deadly calm as she

shifted gears. She glanced in the rearview mirror. "Someone's been following us since we left the house."

"What?" Gunner glanced over his left shoulder and out the back window. His stomach rolled when she took another turn at sixty miles an hour. This was one of those times he wished he had insisted on driving. Trinity was handling the vehicle well, but he'd feel more comfortable if he were behind the steering wheel.

"Looks like they're slowing down," Trinity said, more to herself than to him. She decreased her speed, but not by much.

Gunner glanced out the back window again, glad to see the vehicle no longer riding their bumper. He wished he could get a better look at the car, wondering if it were the same one that ran him off the road.

"Does it look like the same vehicle that hit you a few weeks ago?" Trinity asked, as if reading his mind. "You said that it was a dark sedan, right?"

"Yeah, with dark-tinted windows." He looked back again. "So what do you think they're up to? One minute they're on our tail and the next, they're a block behind us."

"I'm not sure, but I want whoever this is caught before I head home, back to LA."

Gunner wanted more than anything for her to think of his home as her home. He just didn't know how to make that a reality.

"I'll just drive around for a while. Make a few turns to see if they have really given up. What I'd like to do is see if we can get a good look at the vehicle and…hold on!" Trinity yelled just before the car rammed into them.

She made a quick left turn like a NASCAR driver on her final lap. Gunner thought she had lost the car behind them when the dark sedan's wheels squealed and the vehicle skidded past the narrow street that Trinity had turned on. His relief was short-lived when he looked back to find the car gaining speed behind them. Trinity made a few more turns that took them back to the main road.

"Why are you slowing down?" Gunner asked, glancing back over his shoulder, his heart thumping wildly in his chest.

"I want to try something."

"Trinity." He emphasized each syllable of her name as he gripped the door handle. "Don't…" The word caught in his throat and he jumped when the car rammed them again.

"Here we go," Trinity whispered. She held tightly to the steering wheel, her back rigid and her focus on the road. The other car eased up on the side of them.

Gunner wiped his sweaty palms down his pant legs and prayed that they would get through this in one piece. He didn't know what she had planned, but as a former cop, he assumed she knew what she was doing. He just held on for the ride.

The other car sped up and moved to Trinity's side of the car.

"Tri…ni…ty," Gunner said slowly, his pulse pounding in his ear. This was definitely the same car that had run him off the road weeks earlier. With the windows being just as dark as theirs were, he knew the driver couldn't tell who was at the wheel of his car. Just as he couldn't tell who was driving theirs.

His heart leaped and a cold shiver shot up his spine when the other car caught up and rammed the side of his vehicle. Trinity swerved right, then left, but straightened the car.

"Damn it!" She accelerated and jerked the steering wheel to the left, bumping the side of the other car.

"Trinity, babe, be careful." Gunner had one hand on the door handle and one on the back of her seat. "There's a curve coming u—"

The car veered sharply to the left. Gunner's palm slapped the dashboard, the seat belt practically choking him. Trinity rammed the side of the other car and the vehicles jockeyed back and forth for control of the road.

We're going to die, Gunner thought as the car swerved. Trinity rode the curve like an expert driver. Before he could catch his breath, she turned the steering wheel sharply and struck the side of the other car with such force that Gunner's head jerked, sending a searing pain down his spine.

The other driver lost control, spinning several times before slamming into a tree.

"Trinity!" Gunner yelled and grabbed hold of the center console and his door handle when they hopped a curb. He looked up in time to see a brick building, dead smack in the middle of their path.

"Ohmygod!" Trinity screamed and slammed on the brakes.

Gunner's heart lodged in his throat. The car skidded across gravel, still traveling too fast to stop in time to miss the building. Gunner instinctively stretched his left arm in front of Trinity and pushed his feet against the floor as if he had the ability to stop the car.

At the last second, Trinity jerked the steering wheel to the left. The vehicle lurched, and their screams pierced the air when the car spun and didn't stop until the back end of the vehicle slammed into the brick building.

Gunner sat with his eyes closed and didn't move. His heart hammered in his chest while he tried to catch his breath, his body feeling as if it had just gone through a washing machine's spin cycle. He was happy to be alive, but afraid to move, sure that every bone in his body had shattered.

Trinity.

His eyes popped open and he bolted forward, only to drop back against his seat when a blinding pain shot through his head.

Damn.

His hands went to his head and his eyes closed until some of the throbbing ceased. After a few deep breaths, he leaned forward, his bones popping with each move.

He glanced over at Trinity and his heart stopped.

"Trinity." Fear strangled his vocal cords. "Trinity!" he yelled when he saw she wasn't moving. He jerked out of his seat belt, ignoring the pain shooting through his body. If anything had happened to her...

"Gunner," she finally said, her voice barely audible.

"Oh, thank God." He kissed her lips and frantically brushed her hair out of her face, relief gliding through him like a breath of fresh air. He had never been very spiritual, but growing up in his parent's home and attending church weekly, he definitely knew how to pray. And right now, he didn't think he could praise God enough for keeping them alive.

He leaned back slightly. Concern gripped him hard when Trinity still hadn't moved and hadn't opened her eyes.

"Are you hurt?" He hurried and released her seatbelt, almost afraid to touch her. "Sweetie, talk to me. Where does it hurt?" His hand swept down the right side of her body and then her left side, hoping that nothing was broken. She flinched and he froze, his hand resting against her ribs.

"I'm okay," she said quickly. A little too quickly. She opened her eyes and met his gaze. "Just banged up a little," she said, her voice raspy, and he could tell she was in pain.

Gunner swallowed hard. All the love he felt for her came crashing down around him like a two-ton boulder. It was because of him that they were even out there in the middle of the night. "Sweetheart, I think you're a little more than banged up." He moved his hand gently against her ribs again and she flinched, her eyes slamming closed.

"Dammit!" He sat back in his seat, a few more curses filling the interior of the car.

He pulled out his phone and called 911, giving his and Trinity's location as well as Maxwell's information, asking that they contact him. The operator requested that he stay on the line, but Gunner couldn't just sit there. He had to know if it was Simon McCallum in that other car. He shoved the car door open and slowly climbed out of the vehicle, allowing his spaghetti legs to adjust to the weight of his body.

"Gunner...please...just wait for the cops."

Gunner stopped and glanced back at Trinity and almost did what she asked until the driver's side door of the other car swung open. He eased away from their vehicle, his legs still shaky. He stopped when he saw the person fighting to get from beneath the airbag that had him trapped.

Gunner heard sirens in the distance as he moved slowly toward the other vehicle. At first, he couldn't get a good look at the person fighting against the airbag, but then the guy stumbled from the car.

Simon. Gunner cursed under his breath. *Trinity was right.*

Simon, one of the best poker players that he had ever played against, took several wobbly steps forward and then he glanced up and met Gunner's angry gaze. Before he could react, Gunner charged at him and tackled him to the ground.

"You low-down son-of-a-bitch!" Gunner roared and smashed his fist into Simon's face over and over again. "You could have killed her, you stupid jerk!" All thoughts of other poker players being hurt and how he had been run down took a backseat to thoughts of Trinity. Gunner couldn't imagine his life without her and tonight he could have lost her.

They rolled around on the ground and punches flew back and forth. An uppercut to his right jaw caught Gunner off guard, but he quickly recovered, sending a jab to Simon's stomach. He wrapped his hands around Simon's neck and squeezed, knocking his head against the ground while Simon pulled at Gunner's hands.

"Stop!" Gunner heard Trinity scream behind him. "Stop!"

Simon head-butted Gunner. Momentarily disoriented, Gunner blinked several times and then lunged at Simon again, hitting him with everything within him. Just as Gunner cocked his arm back to hit Simon again, a loud whistle pierced the air and they froze.

"I said stop, dammit!"

Breathing hard, Gunner pushed away from Simon

and turned, surprised to see Trinity standing over them looking like a young Pam Grier, gun and all. He eyed her warily, her weapon trained on Simon. Gunner hated to admit it, but she looked mad enough to kill either one of them.

Police sirens blared, spearing the quietness of the night, and police cars came from several directions and slid to a stop.

"Drop your weapon!" an officer said from behind Trinity. Gunner stared at her as she held the gun steady, still aimed at Simon. He swallowed hard, unsure of whether she would lay down her gun.

"Sweetheart, he's not worth it. Please lower the gun," Gunner begged. Her gaze met his. He searched her eyes. The anguish he saw sent a bolt of pain straight to his heart and a stab of guilt to his gut.

"Trinity!" Maxwell's voice came from somewhere close, but Gunner didn't see him. His gaze never left the woman he loved. "Trinity, put down your weapon. It's all over, baby," Maxwell said, slowly approaching her.

The moment she handed her gun to her brother, Gunner jumped to his feet and went to her. He pulled her roughly into his arms, almost forgetting about her ribs, and held on as if letting her go would be the death of him.

An hour later, after talking with the police and getting checked out by the paramedics, Gunner approached Trinity, who had also been checked out and questioned separately. She was talking to Maxwell.

When Gunner got closer, Trinity looked in his direction. Everything within him wanted to hold her in his arms and make all of her pain and unhappiness go away. His chest tightened and the heaviness in his heart at that moment reminded him of just what a fool he'd been. He had enough money to last a couple of lifetimes, and could play poker whenever he wanted. But what he felt for Trinity was a once-in-a-lifetime love. He would never find another woman like her again.

He slowed his advance when his gaze met hers and he saw tears in her eyes. He hated the thought of her crying, especially when it was because of him.

"Sorry to interrupt," he said. "But do you mind if I speak to your sister for a minute?"

"Not at all. I'm glad you're all right, man." Maxwell pulled him into a one-arm hug, and then released him. "I have to get going anyway." He turned to Trinity and kissed her on the cheek. "Call me when you get to LA."

"Okay."

Gunner's stomach tightened at the thought of her leaving. He had to figure out a way to get her to give him another chance. Otherwise, he would be following her to Los Angeles, PPO be damned.

"What were you thinking, going after that guy?" Trinity yelled at him. "He could have had a knife…or a gun. You could have been killed," she said, her anger turning into a sob.

Gunner pulled her into his arms, careful of her bruised ribs. "I am so sorry, sweetie," he muttered close to her ear, emotion clogging his throat. "All I could think about is that he could have killed you." Gunner couldn't believe how stupid he'd been over the past few weeks. He knew everything there was to know about poker, and now realized he had a lot to learn when it came to being in love.

Trinity wrapped her arms around his waist, quietly

crying against his chest, gripping the back of his shirt as if it were a lifeline. Despite what they had just experienced, he knew her tears probably had more to do with the way he had treated her lately than the accident.

He kissed the top of her head and sent up a silent "thank you." Not only were their lives spared, but hopefully she would give him a chance to make things right.

"I'm going to LA with you. We have some things to talk about," Gunner said.

Trinity leaned back, her arms still around him, her watery eyes meeting his. "But what about the tournament? You can't leave."

Gunner gently wiped the tears from her cheeks. "I have a pilot on standby who can take us to LA as soon as we get to the airport."

"Gunner, I don't think it's a good idea for you to go. I…" She stopped, took a deep breath and looked away. Fear of losing her gripped Gunner's body.

He touched her chin, gently turning her head to face him. "Then don't leave me, because if you go, I'm going. I know I've acted like a total idiot this past week, but baby, I love you. I love you so damn much."

She looked up at him, her eyes searching his, tears hanging on her eyelashes. "I don't want to leave you. I'm in love with you."

"Aw, sweetheart." He held her face between his hands, relief roaring through his veins. "You don't know how much I needed to hear you say that." He kissed her lips and looked her in the eyes. "You were right. The last few weeks, I've been acting like a complete jerk. When I thought about how I could have lost you in that car crash, I realized how important you are to me." He wiped the tears flowing down her face with the pads of his thumbs. "I will give up poker before I ever let you walk out of my life." He lowered his head and kissed her with a hunger that he felt deep in his soul. She was a part of him. A part that he couldn't live without.

Epilogue

One week later

Excitement flowed around the crowded room. Trinity and Maxwell waited for the PPO representative to officially announce the individuals who would play in its Main Event in November.

Suddenly, cheers and whistles came from every direction and Trinity's hand flew to her chest. Her heart swelled with pride when Gunner was announced as having the highest chip count of the series. She couldn't ever remember being so happy, especially since she knew how hard he'd worked for this goal.

"That son-of-gun did it again." Maxwell applauded along with everyone else. "Not that I'm surprised. He has always excelled at everything, even back in college." Maxwell shook his head and chuckled. "I remember that when we were pledging Omega Psi Phi fraternity, he was line leader and let me tell you, that brotha took his position very seriously."

Trinity smiled, admiring the bond that Gunner and her brother shared. "I can imagine." She glanced around and saw Gunner and several other men heading to the far side of the room.

"I wonder where he's going."

Maxwell followed her gaze. "The winners have to take care of paperwork before they leave."

Trinity looked around the room, surprised to see so many people still there. It had been an interesting two months. She could honestly admit that this assignment had been like no other and she was happy that it was officially over. Since she had agreed to stay in Vegas to see where her and Gunner's relationship went, Connie was more than happy with her new role as vice president of operations, overseeing Layton's Executive Protection Agency in LA.

Trinity turned to Maxwell as a thought popped into her head. "Have you heard anything about Simon Mc-Callum? Did he ever say why he targeted his fellow poker players?

"Supposedly his poker game has been suffering over the past few months. He's also in financial trouble and needed some big wins during the PPO circuit, which didn't happen for him. He thought that by eliminating his toughest opponents, he'd have a better shot at winning one of the nine seats at the final table."

Trinity shook her head. "That's a shame. I can't believe he was desperate enough to do bodily harm to so many people."

"Yeah, I know."

"Excuse me, everyone," the announcer said over the loud speaker. "May I have your attention?" After a few minutes, a hush fell over the room where thousands of people waited to congratulate the winners and their loved ones.

"I can't see. What's happening?" Trinity asked Maxwell as she volleyed from one foot to the other, trying to see past those who were taller. Even in her four-inch heels she wasn't tall enough.

"It looks like they're waiting for someone to come onto the small platform, but…" Maxwell's words died on his lips when Gunner's voice came over the speakers.

"I'm sorry, everyone, for the intrusion."

Trinity searched for a chair. Finding one, she pulled it next to Maxwell and used his shoulder to help her climb onto the seat.

"There are a few things I wanted to say," Gunner started, "but first I'd like to congratulate the other eight finalists."

Cheers went up around the room and it took a while to get everyone to settle down again.

"In addition to that, I have a few things I need to say to someone who is extremely important to me. Trinity Layton." Gunner placed his hand above his eyes like a visor, to glance around the room until he spotted her. "Sweetheart, come up here. Max, help her get through."

Oh, my goodness. Trinity looked wide-eyed at her brother from her spot on the chair.

"You heard the man. Let's go," Maxwell said, humor in his tone. He lent her his hand and helped her step down.

"Wh…what is he doing?"

"I'm sure you'll find out soon enough." Maxwell used his wide shoulders to create a path for them.

Trinity straightened her gold halter top and patted her hair. She hated being the center of attention, yet everyone's gazes bore into her.

A wave of nervousness swept through her when Gunner extended his hand and helped her onto the platform. "Hey, sweetie." He held on to her hand and gave her a lingering kiss on the lips.

"What are you doing?" she said under her breath. He flashed that mischievous grin that she had grown to love.

"Ladies and gentleman, this gorgeous woman is the love of my life. Over the past couple of months we have been through plenty of sh—stuff."

Laughter floated around the room and Trinity couldn't take her gaze off the man who had stolen her heart. The man who saved her agency with his generosity. The man who had vowed to help her fulfill her dream of setting up a homeless shelter in LA and the man who made her forego her professional standards for a chance at love. She wasn't much of a gambler, but this was one gamble she was glad she took.

Gunner turned to face her, love brimming in his eyes. "I meant what I said." He brought her hand up to his lips and kissed the inside of her wrist, sparking goose bumps to crawl up her arm. "I will give up poker if it means not having you in my world."

Trinity cupped her hand against his cheek, forgetting that hundreds of people were watching. "I will never, *ever* ask you to give up something you love."

"Sweetheart, I love you. I can't imagine living the rest of my life without you in it. I know it won't be easy, but I'm hoping you can find it in your heart to put up with my unique line of work. I'm also hoping that you'll be able to tolerate my overprotective nature." A few chuckles came from the crowd.

Gunner released her hand and placed the microphone back into the mic stand, before pulling a small blue box from his pocket.

Trinity thought her heart would burst from the love she felt for him, especially when he dropped down on one knee. Tears streamed down her face as he opened the box and revealed a round platinum five-carat diamond. The exquisite ring had smaller diamonds around the large center diamond, as well as stones along each side.

"Trinity Marie Layton, will you marry me?"

"Yes! Yes, baby, I'll marry you!"

He stood and slipped the diamond onto her ring finger, and then his arms went easily around her waist, careful of her bruised ribs. Gunner covered her mouth with his and Trinity felt as if she would melt within his embrace. His kiss was so sweet and tender, it was easy to block out everything and everybody, including the clapping and whistling coming from the large crowd.

Trinity had dreamed of how it would be when a man asked for her hand in marriage, but Gunner exceeded all of her expectations. She had no idea this type of happiness existed. All she knew was that she was going to spend the rest of her life making sure that this man knew how much she loved him.

Gunner reluctantly broke off the kiss and lifted his head, staring into her teary eyes. "I'm glad you said yes, because I'm going to need you to guard my body for the rest of our lives."

* * * * *

He wasn't looking for romance…then he met her.

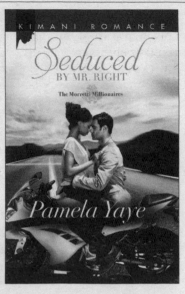

KIMANI ROMANCE

Seduced BY MR. RIGHT

The Morretti Millionaires

Pamela Yaye

Seduced BY MR. RIGHT

Pamela Yaye

Race car legend Emilio Morretti stunned the world when he walked away from his fabulous career after a heartbreaking tragedy. He isn't looking for redemption or romance when he meets Sharleen Nichols, who is haunted by her own painful secret. Yet the voluptuous life coach's infectious zeal is starting to make him feel like a winner again. But will an enemy's vendetta destroy the happiness finally within their reach?

The Morretti Millionaires

HARLEQUIN®
www.Harlequin.com

Available March 2015!

KPPY3930315

The man who
always gets what he
wants is embracing
his biggest challenge
yet…

AlTonya
Washington

After a painful relationship, Vectra Bauer is looking for a no-strings
fling with Qasim Wilder, her platonic friend and financial advisor.
But settling for a little of anything isn't Sim's ideal. He can't
understand why she's hiding from their intense connection that's way
more than just physical. His challenge: to make the woman he adores
believe in love once more…

Available March 2015!

They have
an undeniable
attraction....

SNOWY
MOUNTAIN
NIGHTS

LINDSAY
EVANS

The last person Reyna Allen expects to run into while vacationing is
Garrison Richards, her ex-husband's divorce lawyer. Garrison is good
at his job—a little too good—but he wants to show Reyna that he has
since found his moral compass. But as their mutual heat thaws her
resolve, will doubts put the freeze on their relationship before he can
convince her that they're meant for happily-ever-after?

**"The author has exceptional skills in painting the scenery, making it
easy for readers to visualize the story as it unfolds."
—RT Book Reviews on PLEASURE UNDER THE SUN**

Available March 2015!

REQUEST YOUR FREE BOOKS!

2 FREE NOVELS
PLUS 2 FREE GIFTS!

KIMANI™
ROMANCE

Love's ultimate destination!

Two classic novels featuring the sexy and sensational Westmoreland family…

SPARKS OF TEMPTATION

New York Times
Bestselling Author
BRENDA JACKSON

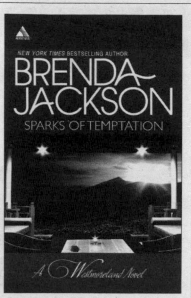

The moment Jason Westmoreland meets Bella Bostwick in *The Proposal*, he wants her—and the land she's inherited. With one convenient proposal, he could have the Southern beauty in his bed and her birthright in his hands. But that's only if Bella says yes…

The affair between Dr. Micah Westmoreland and Kalina Daniels ended too abruptly. Now that they are working side by side, he can't ignore the heat that still burns between them. And he plans to make her his… in *Feeling the Heat*.

Available now!

HARLEQUIN®
TM www.Harlequin.com

KPBJ1700215R

It may be the biggest challenge she's ever faced...

NAUGHTY

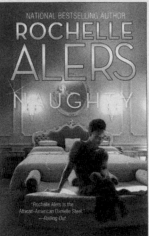

National Bestselling Author

ROCHELLE ALERS

Parties, paparazzi, red-carpet catfights and shocking sex tapes—wild child Breanna Parker has always used her antics to gain attention from her R & B–diva mother and record-producer father. But now, as her whirlwind marriage to a struggling actor implodes, Bree is ready to live life on her own terms, and the results will take everyone—including Bree—by surprise.

"Rochelle Alers is the African-American Danielle Steel."
—*Rolling Out*

"This one's a page-turner with a very satisfying conclusion."
—*RT Book Reviews on SECRET VOWS*

Available now!

KPRA1690115R